Family Affair

BY DEBBIE MACOMBER

Angels Everywhere
Christmas Angels
Mrs. Miracle
Sooner or Later
Someday Soon
The Trouble with Angels
One Night
A Season of Angels
Morning Comes Softly

Family Affair

Debbie Macomber

DOUBLEDAY LARGE PRINT HOME LIBRARY EDITION

WILLIAM MORROW
An Imprint of HarperCollins*Publishers*

Originally published in 1994 as "Family Affair" in *Purrfect Love* by HarperMonogram, an imprint of HarperCollins Publishers.

"Homemade Treats for Your Cat" appears courtesy of PetPlace.com.

First William Morrow edition published 2011.

ISBN 978-1-61129-088-2

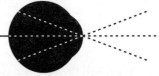

This Large Print Book carries the
Seal of Approval of N.A.V.H.

To Denise Weyrick
for her love, kindness,
dedication to family and friends,
and courage

January 2010

Dear Friends,

Several years ago I was asked to write a story involving a cat. No problem. As it happened our children have owned several cats through the years. Wayne's and my first pet was a cat named, appropriately enough, Kitty. For the first few years of our marriage it was Cats "R" Us. Then, along with the children, came the hamsters, guinea pigs, several dogs, a snake or two, an injured crow, and even a horse. That was when the household became Animals "R" Us. Four children, born within five years, and an entire menagerie of pets . . . oh, those were the days!

I titled my story *Family Affair* for reasons you will come to understand once you start reading. The book made a small blip in the publishing world and then was laid to rest in the out-of-print section of some computer database until now. . .

Apparently my cat Cleo, the heroine of *Family Affair,* has more than one life. Cleo is back and eager to share her story with you. As you'll soon discover, love in the cat world is almost as complicated as it is with humans.

I hope you enjoy this romantic comedy, raised from the ashes like the phoenix to live and charm again. Pour yourself a cup of tea, cuddle up in a comfortable chair, and if one is at hand, put a cat in your lap to pet while you're reading. I always found it comforting to hold an animal in my lap.

I enjoy hearing from my readers. You can reach me through my web site at www.DebbieMacomber.com or by writing me at P.O. Box 1458, Port Orchard, WA 98366.

Warmest regards,
Debbie Macomber

One

"I've got the backbone of a worm," Lacey Lancaster muttered as she let herself into her apartment. She tossed her mail onto an end table and glared at Cleo. "I didn't say a word to Mr. Sullivan, not a single word."

Cleo, her Abyssinian cat, affectionately wove her golden-brown body between Lacey's ankles. Her long tail coiled around Lacey's calf like a feather boa, soft, sleek, and soothing.

"I had the perfect opportunity to ask for a raise and did I do it?" Lacey demanded, kicking her feet so that her shoes sailed in opposite directions. "Oh, no, I let it pass by. And do you know why?"

Cleo apparently didn't. Lacey took off her bright green vinyl raincoat, opened the closet door, and shoved it inside. "Because I'm a coward, that's why."

Walking into the kitchen, she opened the refrigerator and stuck her head inside, rooting out some sorry-looking leftovers, two boxes of take-out Chinese, and the tulip bulbs she'd meant to plant in her balcony flower box last October.

"I'm starved." She opened the vegetable bin and took out a limp stalk of celery. "You know my problem, don't you?"

Cleo meowed and wove her way between Lacey's ankles once more.

"Oh, sorry. You're probably hungry too." Lacey reached inside the cupboard and pulled out a can of gourmet cat food. To her surprise, Cleo didn't show the least bit of interest. Instead, she raised her tail and stuck her rear end in the air.

"What's going on with you? Trust me, Cleo, this isn't the time to go all weird on me. I need to talk." Taking her celery stick with her, she moved into the living room and fell onto the love seat.

"I work and slave and put in all kinds

of overtime—without pay, I might add—
and for what? Mr. Sullivan doesn't appreciate me. Yet it's *my* decorating
ideas he uses. The worst part is, he
doesn't even bother to give me the
credit." She chomped off the end of the
celery and chewed with a vengeance.
The stalk teetered from the attack and
then slowly curved downward.

Lacey studied the celery. "This might
as well be my backbone," she muttered. Unable to sit still any longer,
she paced her compact living room. "I
haven't had a raise in the whole year
I've worked for him, and in that time
I've taken on much more responsibility and completed projects Mr. Sullivan
couldn't or wouldn't do. Good grief, if
it weren't for me, Mr. Sullivan wouldn't
know what was going on in his own
business." By this time she was breathless and irate. "I do more work than he
does, and he's the owner, for heaven's
sake!"

Clearly Cleo agreed, because she
let out a low, wailing moan. Lacey had
never owned a cat before, but after
a devastating divorce she'd needed

someone. Or some thing. The thing had turned out to be Cleo.

She'd first spotted Cleo in a pet-shop window, looking forlorn. Cleo's brother and sister had been sold two weeks earlier, and Cleo was all alone. Abandoned, the half-grown kitten gazed, dejected and miserable, onto the world that passed her by.

Lacey had been suffering from the same emotions herself, and once they met the two had become fast friends. No fool, the pet-store owner knew a sale when he saw one. He'd made some fast soft-shoe moves to convince Lacey what a good investment Cleo would be. If she bred her and sold off the litter, within a year or so, he claimed, her original investment would be returned to her.

Lacey hadn't been so keen on the breeding aspect of the deal, but it had sounded like something she should try. She wanted companionship, and after her disastrous marriage she was through with men. A cat wouldn't lie or cheat or cause hurt. Peter had done all three with bone-cutting accuracy.

Good ol' Peter, Lacey mused. She should be grateful for all the lessons he'd taught her. Perhaps someday she would be able to look back on her marriage without the crushing pain she felt now. He'd vowed to love and cherish her but then calmly announced one Sunday afternoon, without warning, that he was leaving her for someone else.

Someone else was a tall blonde with baby blue eyes and a voluptuous figure. Lacey had sized up the competition, decided she didn't stand a chance, and signed the divorce papers. Oh, there'd been some haggling, but she'd left that to her attorney and stayed out of it as much as possible. As soon as her divorce was final, she'd uprooted herself, moved to San Francisco, located a job she loved, and started life all over again.

Sort of.

This time, she was playing it smart. Men were completely out of the picture. For the first time, she was supporting herself. For the first time, she didn't need anyone else. Because it could happen all over again. Another blonde with a *Playboy* figure could disrupt her life a second time. It was best to play it safe. Who needed that kind of grief? Not her!

Lacey wasn't discounting her assets. With her straight brown hair sculpted around her ears, and equally dark eyes, she resembled a lovable pixie. She was barely five feet tall, while her brother, who was five years older, was nearly six feet. Why nature had short-changed her in the height department, she would never understand.

After the divorce, Lacey had felt emotionally battered and lost. Bringing Cleo into her life had helped tremendously, so much that Lacey figured she could do without a man. Her cat provided all the companionship she needed.

"Okay, okay, you're right," Lacey said, glancing down at her fidgeting feline friend. "I couldn't agree with you more. I'm a gutless wonder. The real problem is I don't want to quit my job. All I'm looking for is to be paid what I'm worth, which is a whole lot more than I'm making now." She'd come out of the divorce with a hefty settlement; otherwise she'd be in dire financial straights.

Cleo concurred with a low wail, unlike any sound Lacey could ever remember her making.

Lacey studied her cat. "You all right, girl? You don't sound right."

Cleo thrust her hind end into the air again and shot across the room to attack her catnip mouse. Whatever was troubling her had passed. At least Lacey hoped it had.

Muttering to herself, Lacey returned to the kitchen and reexamined the contents of her refrigerator. There wasn't anything there she'd seriously consider eating. The leftover Chinese containers were filled with hard, dried-out rice and a thick red sauce with what had once been sweet-and-sour pork. The meat had long since disappeared, and the sauce resembled cherry gelatin. The only edible items were the tulip bulbs, not that she'd seriously consider dining on them.

She'd hoped to treat herself to something extravagant to celebrate her raise. Domino's Pizza was about as extravagant as she got. But she wasn't doing any celebrating this night. If she wanted dinner, she'd need to fix it herself.

Her cupboards weren't promising: a couple of cans of soup mingled with fifteen of gourmet cat food.

Soup.

Her life had deteriorated to a choice between cream of mushroom and vegetarian vegetable. Blindly she reached for a can and brought out the vegetable. The freezer held a loaf of bread. Her choice of sandwiches was limited to either peanut butter and jelly or grilled cheese.

"Sometimes I think I hate you!" The words came through the kitchen wall as clearly as if the person saying them were standing in the same room.

Lacey sighed. Her neighbor, Jack Walker, and his girlfriend were at it again. She hadn't formally met the man who lived next door, which was fine with her. The guy suffered from severe woman problems; from what she'd heard through the wall, it sounded as if the pair was badly in need of therapy. Lacey avoided Jack like the plague, despite his numerous attempts at striking up an acquaintance. She was polite but firm, even discouraging. She had to give him credit. He didn't accept *no* easily. Over the months, his methods had become increasingly imaginative. He'd tried flowers, tacked notes to her door, and had once attempted to lure her into his apartment with the offer of dinner. Of all his tactics, the promise of a meal had been the most tempting, but Lacey knew trouble when she saw it and resisted.

As far as she was concerned, dating Jack was out of the question, especially since he was already involved with someone else. Lacey had lost count of the times she'd heard him arguing with his girlfriend. Some nights she was forced to turn on her stereo to block out the noise.

But being the polite, don't-cause-problems sort of person she was, Lacey had never complained. She might as well throw herself down on the carpet and instruct people to walk all over her.

"I wasn't always a worm," she complained to Cleo. "It's only in the last year or so that I've lost my self-confidence. I'd like to blame Mr. Sullivan, but I can't. Not when I'm the one who's at fault. You'd think it'd be easy to ask for a little thing like a raise, wouldn't you? It isn't, yet I'm left feeling like Oliver Twist. At least he had the courage to ask for more.

"Mr. Sullivan should thank his lucky stars. I'm good at what I do, but does he notice? Oh, no. He just takes me for granted."

Having finished this tirade, she noticed that Cleo had disappeared. Even her cat had deserted her. She found Cleo on the windowsill, meowing pathetically.

Lacey lifted the cat in her arms and petted her. "Have I been so wrapped up in my own problems that I've ignored you?"

Cleo leaped out of the embrace and raced into the bedroom.

The arguing continued in the other apartment.

"Sarah, for the love of heaven, be reasonable!" Jack shouted.

"Give it to him with both barrels," Lacey said under her breath. "I bet you didn't know Jack was dating on the side, did you? Well, don't get down on yourself. I didn't know what a womanizer Peter was either."

Sarah apparently heeded her advice, because the shouting intensified. Jack, who generally remained the calmer of the two, was also losing it.

If she listened real hard, she might be able to figure out the cause of their dispute, but frankly Lacey wasn't that interested.

"I saw him with someone new just last week," she added, just for fun. Lacey had bumped into Jack at the mailbox. There'd been a woman with him and it wasn't Sarah. But it was always Sarah who came back. Always Sarah he quarreled with. The poor girl apparently cared deeply for him. More fool she.

"I'm having vegetarian vegetable soup," Lacey informed Cleo as she strolled into the room, thinking her pet would want to know. "It isn't anything that would interest you, unfortunately." Whatever had been troubling her cat earlier was under control for the moment.

Dinner complete, Lacey set her steaming bowl of soup and her grilled cheese sandwich on the table. She'd just sat down when something hit the wall in the apartment next door. Instinctively, she jumped.

Angry voices escalated. Jack was no longer calm and in control. In fact, it sounded as if he'd lost his cool completely. The two were shouting at each other, each trying to drown the other out.

Lacey sighed. Enough was enough. Setting her napkin aside, she went over to the kitchen wall and knocked politely. Either they didn't hear her or they chose to ignore her, something they did with increasing frequency.

She'd just sat down again when an explosion of noise nearly jerked her off the chair. One or the other of the disgruntled lovers had decided to turn on the radio. Full blast.

The radio was turned off as abruptly as it had been turned on, followed by a tirade from Jack.

The radio was switched back on.

Off.

Once again, ever so politely, Lacey tapped the wall.

They ignored her.

Then, for whatever reason, there was silence. Blissful silence. Whatever had plagued the two was settled. Either that or they'd murdered one another. Whichever it was, the silence was bliss.

When Lacey had finished her dinner, she washed the few dishes she'd used. Cleo continued to weave her sleek body between Lacey's ankles, meowing and wailing all the while. "What's wrong with you, girl?" Lacey asked again.

Squatting down, she ran her hand over the cat's spine. Cleo arched her back and cried once more.

"You don't seem to be yourself," Lacey commented, concerned.

It hit her then, right between the eyes. "You're in heat! Oh, my goodness, you're in heat." How could she have been so obtuse?

Leaving the kitchen, she rooted through her personal telephone directory, searching for the name the pet-shop owner had given her. If she was going to breed Cleo, she needed to talk to this woman first.

"Poor, poor Cleo," Lacey said sympathetically. "Trust me, sweetie, men aren't worth all this trouble." She quickly located the phone number and punched it out.

"I'm Lacey Lancaster," she said hurriedly into the receiver. "The owner of Pet's World gave me your number. I bought an Abyssinian several months ago."

No sooner had she introduced herself when the arguing in the next-door apartment resumed.

"I'm sorry, dearie, but I can't understand you." The woman on the other end of the line spoke with a soft Irish accent.

"I said I purchased an Abyssinian cat—"

"It sounds like you've a party going on."

"There's no party." Lacey spoke louder, close to shouting herself.

"Perhaps you should call me back when your guests have left," came the soft Irish brogue. With that the line was disconnected.

Something snapped in Lacey. Her never-cause-a-scene upbringing went down the drain faster than tap water. She slammed the phone down and clenched her fists.

"I've had it!" she shouted. And she had. With men who didn't know the meaning of the words "faithful" and "commitment." With employers who took advantage of their employees. With Neanderthal neighbors, who shuffled one woman after another through their apartments without a second thought.

Lacey walked out her door and down the hall, her strides eating up the distance in seconds. However, by the time she reached Jack's apartment the fire had died down. Her anger would solve nothing. She tapped politely and waited.

The arguing stopped abruptly and the door flew open. Lacey was so astonished that she leaped back. Sarah leaped back, too, and glared at her. It was apparent the other woman hadn't heard Lacey knock.

"Hello," Lacey said, her heartbeat roaring in her ears. "I was wondering if you two would mind holding it down just a little bit."

The woman, young and pretty, blinked back tears. "You don't need to worry. I was just leaving!"

Jack appeared then, looking suave and composed. He brightened when he saw it was her. "Lacey," he said, flashing her an easy grin. "This is a pleasant surprise."

"With all your fighting, I couldn't even make a phone call," she explained, not wanting to give him the wrong impression. This wasn't a social visit.

"I apologize." Jack glared at Sarah. "It won't happen again."

Sarah's chin shot into the air as she jerked her purse strap over her shoulder. "I . . . I don't believe we have anything more to say to each other." She hurried past Lacey toward the elevator.

"Sarah." Jack placed both his hands on Lacey's shoulders and edged his way past her. "I'm warning you . . . just don't do anything stupid."

"You mean, like listen to you?"

Jack groaned and stared at Lacey as if this were all her fault.

Lacey opened her mouth to tell him exactly what she thought of him and then abruptly changed her mind. Jack wouldn't listen. Men never did. Why waste her breath?

With nothing more to say, she returned to her apartment. To her surprise she realized she'd left the door open. Her immediate concern was for Cleo, and she rushed inside in a panic.

She stopped cold in her tracks at the sight that greeted her.

"Cleo!" Her cat was in the throes of passion with a long-haired feline she didn't recognize.

Placing her hands over her mouth,

Lacey sagged against the wall. She wasn't going to need the Irish woman after all. Cleo had already found her mate.

Two

"Stop!" Lacey demanded, already knowing it was too late. The two cats ignored her. So much for the thrill of being a cat owner.

Knowing only one thing to do, Lacey raced into the kitchen and filled a tall glass with water. She'd get the lovers' attention soon enough. Rushing back into the living room, she tripped on a throw rug and staggered a few steps in a desperate effort to maintain her balance. By the time she reached the cats, most of the liquid was down the front of her blouse and only a few drops landed on the passionate couple.

By then they were finished and the strange cat was looking for a way out of her apartment. Typical male! He'd gotten what he wanted and was ready to be on his merry way.

Lacey was about to open the sliding glass door that led out to her balcony when someone rang her doorbell. Frowning fiercely at the alley cat, Lacey traipsed across her living room and checked the peephole.

It was her Don Juan neighbor, fresh from his argument with Sarah. "Hello again." He flashed her an easy smile which, Lacey hated to admit, hit its mark. She didn't know what was in her personality profile that made her vulnerable to this type of man, but whatever it was, she sincerely wished it would go away.

"I don't suppose you've seen my cat?" he asked.

"You own a cat?"

"Actually, he allows me to live with him."

As if she'd planned it this way, Cleo strolled past, her tail in the air, giving the impression of royalty. The long-haired mixed breed followed closely behind, looking as if he'd rested enough for a second go-round.

"There's Dog," Jack said.

"Dog? You named your cat Dog?"

"Yeah," he said, walking past her. He reached for his cat affectionately and cradled him in his arms. "I wanted a dog, but I had to compromise."

"So you got yourself a cat named Dog." In light of how she'd met his faithful companion, Lacey wasn't amused.

"Exactly."

"Well, listen here, your Dog has stolen Cleo's virginity. What do you plan to do about it?"

Jack's eyes widened. Lacey swore the man looked downright pleased. "Dog? What do you have to say for yourself?"

"It's you I'm asking," Lacey said, squaring her shoulders. "As a responsible pet owner, you have an answer, I hope."

His dark eyes narrowed. "I can only apologize."

"Then I accept your apology," Lacey murmured. It seemed darn little in light of the possible consequences, but the less they had to say to each other the better. Lacey wanted as little to do with Jack as possible. The more she saw of him the more attracted she was, which made absolutely no sense. She was like someone on a strict diet, irresistibly drawn to a dessert tray.

"Listen, I was hoping for an opportunity to get to know you a little better," Jack said, as if he planned to stay awhile.

Lacey couldn't allow that to happen. She all but opened the door for him.

"We've been neighbors for the past several months. I think we must have gotten started on the wrong foot," he said, showing no signs of leaving. "I understand you aren't interested in dating, but we could be a bit more neighborly, don't you think?"

Lacey nodded politely, if reluctantly. It would help to have someone to feed her cat and collect her mail on occasion. She would be willing to do the same for him, but she wanted it firmly understood that this was the extent of what she was offering.

She told him so.

"Friends?" he asked, holding out his hand.

"Friends," she agreed. They exchanged handshakes. She found his grasp secure, but his fingers held hers far longer than necessary. She disliked the way her heart reacted. This man was dangerous in more ways than one. The less she had to do with him, the better.

He seemed to be waiting for her to invite him to stay for coffee and chit-chat. The thought was tempting. It would be nice to have someone to be neighborly with, but the lesson she'd learned from Peter had sunk in.

"We do seem to share a love of cats," Jack added, as if this were grounds for a long-standing friendship.

"I like Cleo," she said pointedly. "Now if you'll excuse me." This time she held the door open for him.

"It was nice talking to you, Lacey," Jack said with a boyish grin that was potent enough to topple her resolve to limit their relationship. "I'm hoping we can become *good* friends."

Lacey didn't miss the emphasis on *good*. The last thing she needed or wanted was friendship with a known Casanova. Not when she'd been fool enough to marry one who'd ruthlessly left her for another.

Since she hadn't summoned the gumption to ask for a raise, she found it even more difficult to explain to her neighbor that she wasn't interested in a man who kept women on the side.

Jack left then, to Lacey's intense relief. She scooped Cleo up in her arms and held her tight, as if her beloved cat had had a narrow escape. Cleo, however, didn't take kindly to being pressed against a wet blouse and squirmed free, leaping onto the carpet. She made her way to the seat of the overstuffed chair, her favorite spot for a catnap, and curled up contentedly. It might have been Lacey's imagination, but Cleo seemed completely at ease and thoroughly satisfied.

Just as Lacey was about to turn on the television, the phone rang. It was probably her best friend, Jeanne Becker. Jeanne had been one of the first people to befriend Lacey after her move to San Francisco. She worked as a dental assistant and was single, like Lacey, but had been dating Dave steadily for nearly a year. However, neither seemed to be in any hurry to get engaged. With so many friends divorcing, they both wanted to be very sure they were taking the right step.

"Well?" Jeanne asked. "Did you ask for your raise?"

"No," Lacey confessed.

"Why not?" Jeanne demanded. "You promised you would. What's so difficult about talking to Mr. Sullivan?"

"I have no defense. I'm a worm."

"What are you so frightened of?" Jeanne asked after a thoughtful moment, as if there were something deep and dark hidden in Lacey's childhood that kept her from confronting her employer.

"I don't know," Lacey admitted. "It's just that Mr. Sullivan is so . . . so intimidating. He's got these beady eyes, and when I ask to talk to him, he looks at his watch as if he doesn't have any time for me and asks how long it will take. And by the time he goes through this little routine, I've lost my nerve."

"Don't you know the man's psyching you out?"

"Yeah, I suppose," Lacey murmured, disheartened. "But knowing that doesn't do any good. My talk with Mr. Sullivan isn't the only thing that went wrong," she added. "Cleo's in heat, and the neighbor's cat stole into my apartment, and I found them . . . together."

"Oh, dear, it sounds like you've had a full day."

"It gets better," Lacey said. "The guy who lives next to me suggested we be neighborly."

"You mean the hunk who's been asking you out for the last six months? I met him, remember?"

Lacey wasn't comfortable thinking of Jack in those terms, but she let her friend's comment pass. "Yeah. He owns Dog, the cat who had his way with Cleo. And before you ask, I did get the name of his cat right."

"I could like this guy," Jeanne said, laughing softly.

"You're welcome to him."

"Lacey! Honestly, when are you going to let bygones be bygones? Peter was a rat, but he's out of your life. The worst thing you can do is blame other men for what happened between you and your ex."

"I'm not blaming other men."

"You've been divorced for over a year now and you never date."

"I don't want another relationship."

"You were wise not to date right away," Jeanne said sympathetically, "but now it's time you got on with your life. If you want my advice, I think you should go out with Jack. He's adorable."

"Are you crazy?" Lacey insisted. "He was fighting with Sarah again. It's all I can do not to tell that sweet young girl what I know. He's playing her for a fool just the way Peter played me."

"You're jumping to conclusions."

"I don't think so," Lacey insisted. "They're constantly fighting. From bits of conversation I've heard, it sounds like Jack wants her to move in with him. Apparently she's on to him because she refuses. I wouldn't trust him either."

"You know what's happened, don't you?" Jeanne asked. "You've gotten to be a cynic. I don't think you realize how much Peter hurt you."

"Nonsense," was Lacey's immediate reply. "He didn't do anything more than teach me a valuable lesson."

❖   ❖   ❖

Lacey didn't sleep well that night. It was little wonder, in light of how her day had gone. The unpleasant run-in with her neighbor continued to plague her. Jack was easygoing and friendly, the kind of man who put people at ease. Not her, though. Lacey's defenses went up whenever he was around her.

As luck would have it, they met in the hallway on their way to work the following morning.

"Off to the coal mines, I see," he said amicably as they made their way to the elevator. He was dressed in a dark three-piece suit, and the only word she could think to describe him was debonair. His smile was wide and charming. Too charming, Lacey decided. His eyes were friendly and warm, the type of eyes a woman remembers for a long time.

"Where do you work?" he asked conversationally as he summoned the elevator.

"Sullivan's Decorating," she answered, without elaborating. Encouraging conversation between them wouldn't be smart. It would be far too easy to be seduced by his magnetism.

"Really? I think that was the firm the bank hired last year when we redecorated."

"We've been involved in several bank renovations," she agreeded evenly. So Jack was a bank executive? Lacey didn't press for information, although she couldn't help being curious.

As if reading her thoughts, he reached inside his suit pocket and handed her a business card. "Come see me if you ever need a loan."

"I will, thank you."

"I'll look forward to having you apply." He smiled down on her and, even knowing what she did about him, her heart fluttered. She was cursed, Lacey mused, destined to be attracted to the wrong kind of men. There was probably some technical name for it, some term psychologists used for women like her. *Nutty* would do, she decided. Tangling her life with his would be downright disastrous.

"Have a good day," Jack said when the elevator opened.

"You too." Her voice was little more than a whisper.

"Say," Jack said, turning back abruptly, as if struck by inspiration. "I don't suppose you'd be free for dinner tomorrow night?"

Instinctively, Lacey stiffened. So he hadn't given up trying. "No . . . I'm sorry, I'm not free," she said. Apparently she conveyed her message because he didn't press her.

He glanced at his watch and frowned. "Perhaps another time."

"Perhaps."

Lacey wasn't making Jack Walker any promises. But she couldn't get the thought of Jack out of her mind all day.

❊   ❊   ❊

The following evening, when Lacey was taking her trash to the chute at the end of the hallway, she ran into Jack a second time, just as he was going out his door.

Taken by surprise, they stopped and stared at each other. He was dressed formally as if for a fancy dinner date. Lacey didn't need to be reminded that he could have been wining and dining her. She'd declined his offhand invitation, but she wished briefly that she'd accepted. Then she decided she was right to refuse. There were probably any number of other women who struck his fancy. Then, too, there was always Sarah. Ever loyal, ever faithful.

"Hello again," Jack said, with his electric smile.

"Hello." Her voice sounded awkward. Stilted.

"How's it going?"

"Fine." She didn't ask about him. The answer was obvious. He looked wonderful. Bank executives shouldn't be this good-looking or this friendly.

"Here, let me help." He took the plastic garbage can out of her hand.

"I can do that." Nevertheless, she was pleased he offered.

"I'm sure you can, but let me play the

role of gentleman. It'd make my mama proud." The smile was back in place, potent enough to melt away the strongest of resolves. Hers, unfortunately, dissolved faster than most.

They went down the hallway together. Lacey took pains to avoid brushing shoulders with him. "Thanks for the help," she said, when they neared her apartment door.

"No problem. I was happy to do it."

She reached for the doorknob, intent on escaping. "Have a good time," she said, turning her back to him.

"I probably won't," he said softly, "especially since I won't be spending the evening with you. I'm destined to sit through a boring dinner meeting. I wish you could have seen your way clear to go with me."

"I—" She was so flustered by his sweet talk she could barely speak. "I'm sure you'll have an enjoyable evening. Will you be seeing Sarah?" she added, not knowing where the courage came to ask the question. Sarah was the one he should have invited, not her.

"Not tonight," he said. "I'm afraid I'm stuck with my assistant."

First he'd invited her, and when she refused he'd asked his assistant. Suddenly Lacey was furious. That was exactly what she expected of someone like Jack. Someone like Peter.

Poor Sarah was destined for a broken heart.

Three

Cleo's pregnant," Lacey moaned as she slumped into the BART seat next to Jeanne two weeks later. "I took her to the vet yesterday afternoon and he confirmed her condition." Lacey was deeply dismayed that her purebred Abyssinian had mated with Jack's tomcat. And her dissatisfaction with her neighbor didn't stop there.

Sarah had stopped by over the past weekend, and the sounds of their argument had come through the walls again. Both had been furious. This time, however, they kept the intensity of their disagreement to a lower pitch, and their fight didn't last long. No more than ten minutes had elapsed before Lacey heard Jack's apartment door slam and Sarah's footsteps hurrying down the hall. Jack had stuck his head out and called after her, but to no avail.

"What are you going to do about Cleo?" Jeanne wanted to know.

"I . . . I haven't decided yet." Several options were open to her, but one thing was certain: she was determined that Jack accept some responsibility.

❧   ❧   ❧

That evening, after work, with her heart in her throat, Lacey approached Jack's door and knocked three times in hard, timed beats.

"Lacey, hello! This is a pleasant surprise."

"Hello," she said stiffly. "Would you mind if I came in for a moment?"

"Not at all. I'd be honored." He stepped aside and let her into the living room, which was more than double the size of her own. "Can I get you something to drink?" he asked.

"Nothing, thanks." She sat down on a white leather sofa and took a small notebook from her purse. "I'm afraid this isn't a social call."

Jack sank into a recliner opposite

her. He perched close to the edge of the seat cushion and braced his elbows against his knees. "Is there a problem?"

"As a matter of fact, there is," Lacey answered. "Dog got Cleo pregnant."

"I see."

"I thought you should know."

"Yes, of course." He looked as if he were entirely in the dark as to what she wanted from him. "Is there something you needed?" he asked after an awkward moment.

How like a man! "Yes," she said, having trouble restraining her irritation. "I want you to do right by my cat."

"Do right? Are you suggesting they marry?"

"Don't be ridiculous!"

"Then what do you mean?"

"It's only fair that you share the expenses with me." She hated the way her voice trembled. "Dr. Christman, Cleo's vet, prescribed expensive vitamins and another checkup. In addition, I'll expect you to find homes for your half of the litter."

"My half."

"Yes. Please submit the names to me for approval."

Jack scratched the side of his head. "You're serious about this, aren't you?"

That he should question her motives told her everything she needed to know about him. "Yes, I'm serious. Dead serious." She stood and handed him a list of her expenses so far. "You can pay me whenever it's convenient." Holding her purse against her chest as though it offered her protection, she kept her back ramrod straight. "There are consequences in owning an alley cat, Mr. Walker. Even one named Dog." Lacey knew how pious she sounded. Lines of righteousness creased her face as she let herself out.

She didn't realize how badly she was shaking until she was inside her own apartment. Her knees felt as if they were about to buckle. She sat on the love seat and Cleo leaped into her lap, eager for attention.

Lacey ran her hand down the length of Cleo's back. "Well, girl, you're going to be a mother. What do you think about that?"

Cleo meowed.

"This is destined to be an interesting couple of months," she said. Dr. Christman had given Lacey several pamphlets about the reproduction of cats. Lacey had read them a number of times. She'd grown up with a gentle cocker spaniel named Sherlock, but he'd been a male so she'd never been through this sort of thing.

❧   ❧   ❧

The following afternoon, Lacey's doorbell rang. Jack was on the other side, leaning against the doorjamb. He gave her a slow, easy, heart-stopping grin.

"How's Cleo doing?"

"Fine. She seems to need a bit more attention these days, but other than that she's behaving normally."

"I had Dog neutered. He's keeping a low profile these days."

Lacey was forced to pinch her lips together to keep from smiling. As far as she was concerned, it would do Dog good to have his carousing ways curtailed.

"May I come in?"

Lacey wasn't sure letting Jack into her apartment was such a good idea. "All right," she said reluctantly, stepping aside.

Then Lacey made the mistake of politely asking if he'd like something to drink, and Jack asked for coffee. Since she didn't have any ready, she was required to assemble a pot.

To her dismay, Jack was intent on helping her. She turned on the water and measured out the coffee grounds, all the while complaining inwardly about her compact kitchen. She couldn't move without touching Jack in some way. When she stood on tiptoe to lift down the mugs, he stepped behind her, the full length of his body pressing against hers.

She felt trapped and silly and unbearably uncomfortable. Worse, she was blushing, although she did everything she could to disguise the effect he had on her.

"It seems only fair if I'm going to share the expenses of Cleo's pregnancy that I have visitation rights," he said casually.

A chill washed over her. "Visitation rights?"

"Yes. I'd like to check on her every now and again to be sure she's doing well."

Lacey wasn't sure this was such a good idea, either, but she couldn't think of any good reason to protest.

"I can assure you Cleo will be well cared for."

"I'm confident she will be, but I'd like to check on her myself."

"All right," she agreed with ill grace.

The coffee finished brewing and she poured them each a cup. Jack took his black and strong, but he waited while Lacey diluted hers with milk before returning to the living room.

Cleo walked regally into the room and without a pause jumped into Jack's lap. Lacey was amazed. Her cat had never been fond of strangers.

"Cleo," Lacey chastised. "Get down."

The cat would have been a fool to do so. Jack was petting her back in long, smooth strokes that left Cleo purring with delight. It was probably like this with every woman he touched. Lacey attempted to scrounge up resentment toward him, and to her amazement found she couldn't.

Instead, the very opposite was happening. It was as if Jack's hands were on Lacey. A series of warm, dizzy sensations began to grow in her. Sexual feelings. Her breath came in little short puffs. She sipped at her coffee and forced herself to look away, anything that would make this feeling disappear. It was much too uncomfortable to remember that part of her nature, the one she'd buried after her divorce and conveniently ignored until Jack walked into her life.

Looking away didn't help. Nothing did.

"Cleo's a beautiful cat," he said in a low, sexy drawl that had Cleo purring and Lacey's heart racing.

"Thank you," she managed.

The tingling feeling spread slowly, inexorably, through her body, leaving her with a need she wouldn't have dared express to another human being. It had been well over a year since a man had held her. Not once in all those months had she missed a man's touch. Until now.

Now it was torture to sit and do nothing. To her dismay, Jack seemed relaxed and in no hurry to leave.

"Have you thought about homes for your half of the litter?" she asked, to make conversation.

"No."

"I . . . I think my friend Jeanne will take one." Her gaze followed the movement of his hand against Cleo's soft fur. The brush of his fingers was light, gentle. A lover's touch. He would be a tender lover, Lacey mused.

She shook her head, needing to clear her mind before it completed the picture of making love with him. Oh, dear heaven, this was more than she could bear.

"Lacey." The sexy drawl was back. "Come here."

"W-why?"

"I want you to feel Cleo's tummy."

"It's much too soon for the kittens," she protested and all but vaulted out of her chair. He knew exactly what he was doing to her and he enjoyed it. Lacey's cheeks flamed.

She hurried into the kitchen. Running the faucet, she filled a sponge and wiped down her spotless counter. If only Jack would leave! But that would be asking for a miracle. He had her on the run and wasn't about to give up.

He moved into the compact kitchen, and she closed her eyes, praying for strength.

"It was nice of you to stop by." She hoped he'd leave before she made a fool of herself.

"Why did you turn down my invitation to dinner?" he asked.

She swore he was only inches behind her, but she didn't dare turn around.

"Lacey?"

She opened the cupboard and brought down a can of cat food. "I don't think it's a good idea for us to become involved."

"Why not?"

"It's fine to be neighborly, but . . ."

"Not too friendly."

"Exactly." Her heart continued to beat at maximum speed, clamoring loudly in her ear. She didn't dare look at him. She couldn't, without his knowing that she wasn't any better off than Cleo was with Dog.

"Turn around and look at me," he instructed her gently, and when she didn't comply he placed his hands on her shoulders and slowly moved her to face him. Then he ran his thumb along the edge of her jaw. "Look at me," he repeated.

Lacey closed her eyes and lowered her head. "I think you should leave."

Using his thumb, he lifted her chin. "Open your eyes."

She had no choice but to do as he asked. Reluctantly her eyes opened and slid effortlessly to his.

"I remember the day you moved in." He spoke softly, clearly. His gaze was as dark and intense as she'd ever seen. "I realized then how badly I wanted to get to know you. There was something vulnerable about you. Something that told me I would need to be patient; and so I've bided my time. It's been a year now and I'm still waiting, but I'm growing restless."

Lacey's throat felt dry, and she doubted she could have spoken even if she'd wanted to. Which she didn't. What could she say? That she'd once trusted someone who'd destroyed her faith in all men?

"Who hurt you?" he asked.

She shook her head, unwilling to answer him.

He took her in his arms then, drawing her into a protective circle, easing her into his embrace. His hold was loose, comforting, seductive.

Lacey wanted to resist, tried to make herself pull away, and found she couldn't.

"I want to kiss you," he whispered, as if he felt he needed to warn her of every move he made for fear she'd bolt and run like a frightened rabbit.

"No." She shook her head wildly from side to side. Somehow she found the resistance to brace her hands against his forearms and push herself away.

He let go of her instantly, but hesistantly. "Why not?" he asked. "I would never hurt you, Lacey. I'd never do anything you didn't want, weren't ready for."

"You must think me a fool," she said, her breasts heaving with the effort it had cost her to walk away from him.

"A fool?"

"You love Sarah."

"Of course I love Sarah."

At least he didn't deny it. "How many other women do you have on a string? Don't answer that; I don't want to know. Just understand one thing. I refuse to be one of them."

"Lacey."

"Please leave." She folded her arms and thrust out her chin defiantly.

"Not until you listen to me."

"You can't say anything that will change my mind."

His laugh mocked her. "Not even when I tell you Sarah's my sister?"

Four

"Your sister!" Lacey repeated, stunned. For a moment she wondered if she could trust Jack to tell her the truth but then decided she could. The intimacy between Jack and Sarah was what had struck her the first time she'd seen them together. It made sense that they were brother and sister.

"Who did you think she was?" Jack demanded. "You assumed Sarah and I were lovers? How could you possibly think something like that?"

"You're constantly fighting, and—"

"Of course we fight, we're siblings. Sarah's living with a man and I don't approve. I wish she'd use the brains God gave her and get out."

"Do you disapprove of their living arrangement or of the young man?" Lacey wanted to know.

"Both. As far as I'm concerned, she's making the biggest mistake of her life. Mom and Dad don't know, and I refuse to hide it from them much longer."

"*That's* the reason you keep insisting she move in with you!" Lacey had caught the gist of their disagreement several times and cheered when Sarah flatly refused him. This new information put a different slant on Sarah's refusal.

"How do you know what we argue about?" he asked, regarding her quizzically.

"You honestly think I can't hear you two? Those walls are made of papier-mâché." Her head was reeling. If Sarah was Jack's sister, that answered a multitude of awkward questions.

Jack stuffed his hands in his pockets and strolled to the far side of the kitchen. His brow creased as if he were deep in thought. "I didn't realize we'd been quite so loud."

"You both certainly seem to have strong feelings on the subject."

"All this time you believed I was two-timing Sarah?"

"What else was I to think?" she asked

defensively. "Besides, there were all those other women."

"What other women?"

"The one I saw you with the other day at the mailbox, for example."

"You mean Gloria?"

"I didn't hear her name. . . . Listen, none of this matters. You're free to date whomever you want. You don't owe me any explanations."

He didn't seem to hear her. "Gloria's a friend, nothing more. We did date a few years back, but it didn't develop into anything. She's seeing someone else now."

"What about your assistant?" Lacey asked, before she could censor the question.

"Mrs. Blake?" He laughed outright. "She's fifty and a grandmother."

Lacey wanted so badly to believe him. "Fifty?"

He nodded. "There's only one woman I've had my eye on for the last several months, and it's you."

"You talk a sweet line, Jack Walker, but I've heard it all before." More times than she cared to count. More times than she wanted to remember.

He raised an eyebrow as he advanced a couple of steps toward her. "If you let me kiss you, who knows? You just might change your mind."

The temptation was strong, stronger than Lacey wanted it to be. "Another time," she said, her heart roaring in her ears as she backed away from him.

Jack looked disappointed. "All right, Lacey, I've been patient this long. I can wait." He checked his watch and sighed. "I'd better get back to my place. I'll stop by later in the week to check on Cleo." He waited as if he half expected her to protest.

She didn't, although she probably should have. Life had taught her that men weren't to be trusted. Everything Jack said was well and good, but she refused to believe he'd been interested in her all these months. No man had that kind of patience. At least none she'd ever met.

Before he left, he took her by the shoulders and gently planted a kiss on her cheek.

❖   ❖   ❖

"Are you going to go out with Jack?" Jeanne asked when they met the next morning. Lacey's arms were loaded down with several large books of carpet samples. She swore they weighed twenty pounds each. Her arms felt like they were about to come out of their sockets.

"I don't know."

Jeanne eyed her speculatively. "Lacey, you can't let an opportunity like this pass you by. As I said before, the guy's a hunk."

"Handsome isn't everything."

"True, but it's a good start. Besides, I *like* Jack."

"You only met him once."

"True, but I liked what I saw."

Lacey didn't have an answer for that. They rode in silence for several moments.

"I see you brought your work home with you again." Jeanne glanced disapprovingly in the direction of the samples.

"We're making a bid for an accountant's office, and I stopped off on my way home last night and let him look over the different carpets and colors."

"More overtime you're not getting paid for," Jeanne murmured. "Did you ever stop to think what Mr. Sullivan would do without you?"

Lacey had given that question ample consideration. Every time she worked up a quote or dealt with a moody customer because Mr. Sullivan was "out of the office at the moment," she had that very thought. "He'd probably find some other schmuck to take my place."

"Don't be ridiculous," Jeanne said. "The man needs you. He knows it, and so do you. What you should do, my friend, is use this to your advantage. We both know you should be making double what you make now."

"Double?"

"I don't know what Scrooge is paying you, but I do know it isn't enough. If you don't say something to him soon, I will."

"Jeanne!"

"Relax. I won't. But it makes me angry the way you let him take advantage of you. I don't know what it is about you that lets him get away with it. Do you enjoy being a victim?"

"No!"

Jeanne shrugged. "Then do something about it."

Her friend was right. More than right. She was acting like a victim. Lacey left the BART station filled with indignation. It lasted until she reached the office.

Unfortunately, the lone elevator was out of order. Lugging the carpet samples with her, Lacey huffed and puffed up three flights of stairs and literally staggered into the office.

Mr. Sullivan glanced up and gave her a look of concern. In his late forties, he was fast going bald, and his blue eyes had faded over the years. His suits were meticulously tailored, though, and he insisted they both maintain a crisp professional image.

Lacey pressed her hand over her heart and slumped into the first available chair.

"Lacey, are you all right?"

She shook her head. She hadn't realized how badly out of shape she was until she'd trekked up those stairs hauling two twenty-pound books of samples.

Mr. Sullivan walked over to the water cooler and drew her a cup of clear cold liquid. "Drink this and you'll feel better."

"Mr. Sullivan . . ."—she was so winded her voice could barely be heard—"we need . . . to talk . . . about my . . . position here."

"Of course. You've done a wonderful job. I owe you a debt of thanks. I realize I've left you with some of the more unpleasant tasks lately, and I hope you'll forgive me for that."

He was a kindly man, she realized. Dissatisfied with her wages, she'd built him up in her mind as an ogre with few redeeming qualities. Much as she'd pictured Jack . . . until recently.

"Overtime?" Her lungs hurt, otherwise she would have elaborated.

He frowned as if he didn't understand her. "Are you saying that over time you'd like to become a full-fledged decorator?"

She nodded, but it was more than that.

"You're wonderfully talented, Lacey. In a couple of years I feel strongly that you'll make it." Having said that, he lifted the heavy sample books, replaced them against the wall, and returned to his desk.

Mumbling under her breath, Lacey walked over to her own desk. No sooner had she removed her jacket than Mr. Sullivan announced he was leaving for the rest of the morning. He didn't tell her where he was headed, which was typical.

❀   ❀   ❀

When Lacey returned to her apartment that evening, the first thing she did was soak in a hot tub. It felt wonderful.

Her day had been hectic. She certainly wasn't in the mood for company when there was a knock on her door. She jerked on a pair of sweats. "Oh, please, make this fast," she muttered as she went to answer it.

Jack stood with Sarah on the other

side. "I thought it was time the two of you met," he said.

"I'm Sarah," the pretty brunette said, holding out her hand. Now that Lacey knew they were brother and sister, it was easy to see the family resemblance. Sarah shared Jack's deep chocolate-brown eyes and thick dark hair.

"Jack said there'd been a misunderstanding." Sarah grinned as if amused.

"Please make yourselves at home," Lacey said, gesturing toward the living room.

Jack needed no further invitation. He helped himself to the love seat, and Cleo immediately snuggled in his lap as if she'd been waiting for his return.

Lacey and Sarah sat down too.

"I'm sorry for all the commotion Jack and I make," Sarah said. "He's pretty stubborn, you know."

"Me?" Jack protested.

"All right, we both are. Since Mom and Dad moved to Flagstaff, he's the only family I have here in San Francisco. We fight a lot, but we're close too."

"We'd argue a lot less if it wasn't for

Mark," Jack said with a frown, eyeing his sister.

Sarah's jaw went tight. "Jack, please, you promised not to bring him up. At any rate," she continued, "I wanted to clear up any misconceptions you might have about me. Jack really is my brother."

"I should have realized that. There's a strong family resemblance."

Sarah stood. "I really need to go—Mark's meeting me for dinner—but I wanted to stop by and introduce my-self. Jack's mentioned you several times and—well, I hope everything works out—with Cleo." She squeezed the last two words together in her rush to clarify her meaning.

Sarah left, but Jack stayed exactly where he was—on her love seat with Cleo snoozing contentedly in his lap. "All right," he said, after Lacey had seen Sarah to the door. "What's wrong?"

"What do you mean?"

"Something's troubling you," he said evenly, studying her.

Uncomfortable under his scrutiny, she debated whether or not to tell him the truth. The hot bath hadn't helped to soothe her mind the way she had hoped, and she couldn't stop thinking about what Jeanne had said about her choosing to be a victim.

"I'm a worm," she confessed, slumping in her chair.

"A worm," Jack repeated slowly, as if he wasn't sure of the word's meaning. "In what way?"

She tossed her hands in the air, not wanting to discuss it. The more she complained, the worse she felt. If she was going to whine about her job, she should be doing it to Mr. Sullivan. So far he was the last person to know how she felt, and she had no one to blame but herself.

"All right, you're a worm," Jack said, "but even a worm needs to eat. How about dinner?"

"Out?"

"We can order in if you want, but I bet a night in Chinatown would do us both a world of good."

Lacey blinked back her surprise. Jack was asking her to dinner and she found that she longed to accept more than she had wanted anything for a long time. Before she could resurrect a long list of objections, she nodded.

His smile rivaled the northern lights. "Great." Gently he set Cleo aside. "You like Chinese food?"

"I love it. Hot and spicy and lots of it."

"Me too. The spicier the better."

"They can't make it too hot for me," she told him.

He cocked an eyebrow. "Wanna bet?"

Lacey didn't. Jack insisted on a taxi to save hunting for a parking space in crowded Chinatown. Lacey would have been comfortable riding BART. She didn't own a car and her only means of getting around was public transportation. Luckily the City by the Bay had an excellent metro system.

The taxi let them off on Grant Avenue. Lacey loved walking along the busy streets of Chinatown. Goods from the small shops spilled onto the sidewalk, displayed on long narrow tables. The smells tantalized her. Incense blended with simmering duck and mingled with the keen scent of spices that floated in the air. Chinese lanterns lit up the corners.

Jack guided her toward what he claimed was his favorite restaurant, his hand holding hers. Lacey enjoyed being linked with him, so much so that she was almost frightened by the sense of rightness she experienced.

When they approached a steep flight of stairs that looked like something the Maya had constructed deep in the interior of Mexico, Lacey balked.

"It isn't as bad as it looks." Jack placed an arm around her waist. Lacey could deal with the stairs far easier than she could this newfound intimacy. It didn't help that she'd been up and down three flights several times that day. She explained what had happened with the office elevator, and Jack was appropriately sympathetic.

Dinner started with hot and sour soup, followed by pot stickers in hot oil. Jack did the ordering, insisting she try Szechuan chicken, prawns with chili sauce, and hot pepper beef. Every now and again he'd look at her to be sure she approved of his choices.

"We'll never eat all that," she insisted, leaning toward him until her stomach was pressed against the side of the linen-covered table.

"I know," he said, unconcerned. "There'll be plenty of leftovers for later."

It amazed her that they had so much to talk about. He respected her privacy and didn't pry into subjects she didn't want to discuss. He listened and his laugh was easy, and before she knew it she was completely relaxed. Her problems seemed much less important.

Lacey even managed to sample each of the multiple dishes Jack ordered, none of which she'd tasted before. They were so good, it was hard to stop eating.

By the time they left the restaurant, carrying the leftovers, Lacey was full and content. They walked along the crowded streets, stopping now and again to investigate the wares of a souvenir shop. Jack bought her a bar of jasmine-scented soap and a catnip toy for Cleo.

"Tell her it's from Dog," he said.

She smiled up at him. "I will. It's the least he can do."

"The very least," Jack agreed.

She had trouble pulling her gaze away from his. It had been a long time since she'd had such a happy time with a man.

"We'd better head back," Jack said abruptly, waving to flag down a taxi.

"So soon?" she protested, not understanding the swift change in his mood. One moment they were enjoying each other's company, and the next Jack looked as if he couldn't get home fast enough. He turned and looked at her, his eyes burning into hers. "I don't want to leave either."

"Then why are we going?"

"Because I can't go another minute without kissing you, and doing it on the streets of Chinatown might embarrass you."

Five

"Neither spoke on the ride back to the apartment building. Jack paid the driver, took hold of Lacey's hand, and led her into the lobby. The elevator was waiting with the door wide open, and the instant they were inside Jack reached for her.

The moment their lips met, Lacey realized she'd been half crazy with wanting him. His mouth was firm and needy, as needy as her own. Standing on the tips of her toes, she linked her arms around his neck.

When he lifted his mouth from hers, she buried her face in his shoulder. He held her close, rubbing his chin across the crown of her head. His touch was as gentle as she knew it would be. Cleo trusted this touch, savored it. Now it was her turn.

She wanted him to kiss her again, needed him to, so she'd know this was real. Reading her mind, he used his thumb to raise her chin. His eyes met and held her for a breath-stopping moment before he lowered his lips to hers. His mouth was wet and warm, coaxing. Lacey sighed as her emotions churned like the dense fog that swirls around the Golden Gate Bridge.

This was real, she decided. It didn't get any more real than this. One moment she was clinging to him, breathless with wonder, and the next she was battling tears.

"Lacey."

She didn't answer, but freed herself enough to push the button to their floor, to escape as quickly as possible. She didn't want to talk, to explain emotions she didn't understand herself. Shaking from the impact of his touch, she realized how terribly frightened she was.

After Peter had left, she'd been in shock. If she'd examined her pain then, she would have had to acknowledge how deeply he'd wounded her.

Now there was Jack, patient, gentle

Jack, who evoked a wealth of sensation. But she couldn't accept this promise of joy without first dealing with the dull, throbbing pain of her past.

"Lacey," he whispered, keeping his arms loosely wrapped around her waist. "Can you tell me what's wrong?"

She shook her head. An explanation was beyond her. "I'm fine." It was a small white lie. She'd hadn't been fine from the moment she'd learned that Peter was involved with another woman. She felt broken and inadequate. She had never recovered from the crippling loss of the dream she'd carried with her since she was a child, playing love and marriage with paper dolls.

It wasn't supposed to happen like this. Marriage was forever. Love was supposed to last longer than a night, commitment longer than a few months.

All that Lacey had gotten out of her years with Peter was a bitterness buried so deep in her soul that it took the tenderness of another man, one she barely knew, to make her realize what she'd been doing for the past eighteen months.

Silently, Jack walked with her down the hall that led to her apartment. Pausing outside her door, he brushed a tendril of hair from her face, his touch light and nonthreatening.

"Thank you," he whispered, gently pressing his lips to hers.

She blinked. Twice. "Why are you thanking me?"

A smile lifted the edges of his mouth. "You'll know soon enough."

Her hand trembled when she inserted the key. Cleo was there to greet her, clearly unhappy at having been left so long. It took several moments for Lacey to pull herself away from her thoughts.

Setting her purse aside, she wandered into the kitchen. She could hear Jack's movements on the other side, storing the leftovers in the refrigerator. She poured herself a glass of water and smiled when she heard a light tapping sound coming from the wall.

She reached over and knocked back, smiling at their silly game.

"Good night, Lacey," she heard him say.

"Good night, Jack," she whispered, and pressed her flattened palm against the wall, needing this small connection with him, yet fearing it. She was glad he couldn't see what she had done.

❊   ❊   ❊

Lacey couldn't have been more surprised when Sarah Walker entered Sullivan's Decorating two days after her dinner date with Jack.

"Sarah, hello!" Lacey said, standing to greet Jack's sister.

"I hope you don't mind my stopping in unexpectedly like this." Sarah glanced nervously around the crowded shop. Every available bit of space was taken up by sample books, swatches of material, and catalogs.

"Of course not."

"I was wondering if we could meet for lunch one afternoon and talk?"

Lacey was pleased, although surprised. "I'd enjoy that very much."

They agreed on a time the following week, and Sarah chose a seafood restaurant on Fisherman's Wharf, one of Lacey's all-time favorites.

Lacey saw Jack almost every evening that week, never for very long. He had a long list of convenient excuses for dropping in unannounced, easing his way into her life bit by bit. Lacey knew what he was doing, but she didn't mind. He made no attempt to kiss her again and she was grateful, but she didn't expect his patience to last much longer.

"I was divorced over a year ago," she mentioned casually one evening, not looking at him. With Cleo in her lap, Lacey felt secure enough to touch upon the truth.

Jack sat composed and relaxed on her love seat, holding a mug of coffee, his ankle resting on his knee. "I guessed as much," he said. "Do you want to talk about it?"

"Not now. Do you mind?"

It took him awhile to answer; it seemed like the longest moment of Lacey's life. "No, but I do feel we should. Someday. The sooner the better."

She knew he was right. For the past few days, she had been rewriting her journal. It was the only way she had of sorting out her feelings. The habit of keeping a record of events in her life had started while she was still in school, and for years she had written a paragraph or two at the end of each day.

After Jack kissed her, she'd gone back to the daily journal she'd kept through those painful months before her divorce. What amazed her was the lack of emotion in those brief entries. It was as if she had jotted down the details of a police report. Just the facts, nothing more. Bits and pieces of useless information while her world blew up in her face.

She'd reread one day at a time, and then with raw courage she rewrote those trauma-filled weeks, reliving each day, refusing to dull the pain. What surprised her was the incredible amount of anger she experienced. Toward Peter. And toward Michelle, the woman he'd left her to marry.

The bitterness spilled out of her pen until her hand ached and her fingers throbbed, but still she couldn't stop. It was as if the pen insisted she get it all down as quickly as possible because only then would she be well, only then could she move forward with her life.

She was afraid she was going to explode. Even Cleo knew not to come near her. Holding a box of tissues, she'd weep and pace and weep some more. Then she'd wipe her eyes, blow her nose, and toss the damp tissue willy-nilly. In the morning, she discovered a trail that reached to every room of her apartment.

Sleep avoided her. It wasn't fair. She'd purged her soul, or so she thought. Yet it was well after midnight before she'd fall into a fitful sleep.

Lacey wasn't in the mood for company the next evening when Jack arrived, but she was pleased he'd stopped by. He was easy to be with, undemanding and supportive.

Cleo jumped down from her position in Lacey's lap and strolled into the bedroom, as if she hadn't a care in the world. When Cleo left, Jack stood and moved to Lacey. He stretched out his hand to her.

She looked up at him and blinked

and then, without question, gave him her hand. He clasped it firmly in his own and then lifted her from her chair. Deftly he switched position, claiming her seat, and drew her into his lap.

"You look tired." His gaze was warm and concerned.

"I'm exhausted." As well she should be after the restless night she'd spent. No matter how hard she tried, she couldn't bury the past. It prickled her like stinging nettles.

He eased her head down to his shoulder. "Are you able to talk about your marriage yet?"

It took several moments for Lacey to answer, and when she did she found herself battling back tears. "He fell in love with someone else. He'd been having an affair for months. Oh, Jack, how could I have been so stupid not to have known, not to have realized what was happening? I was so blind, so in-credibly naive."

Jack's hand was in her hair. "He was a fool, Lacey. You realize that, don't you?"

"I . . . all I know is that Peter's happy

and I'm miserable. It isn't fair. I want to make him hurt the way he hurt me." She buried her face in his chest.

When her sobs subsided, Lacey realized Jack was making soft, comforting sounds. Wiping the moisture from her face, she raised her head and attempted a smile.

"Did you understand anything I said?"

"I heard your pain, and that was enough."

Appreciation filled her. She didn't know how to tell him all that was in her heart. How grateful she was for his friendship, for showing her that she'd anesthetized her life, blocked out any chance of another relationship. Little by little, he'd worn down her resistance. All she could think to do was thank him with a kiss.

It had been so very long since a man had held her like this. It had been ages since anyone had stirred up the fire deep within her. Their mouths met, shyly at first, then gaining in intensity. After only a few seconds, Lacey was drowning in a wealth of sensation.

A frightening kind of excitement took hold of her. It had been like this when Jack had kissed her that first time, but even more so now. She opened to him and sighed with surprise and delight as his hold around her tightened. Her initial response was shy.

"Lacey," he groaned, "do you have any idea how much you tempt me?"

"I do?" She basked in the glow of his words. After Peter, she'd been convinced no man would ever find her desirable again.

"We have to stop now."

Lacey had never meant for their kissing to develop to this point, but now that it had, she had few regrets. "Thank you," she whispered and lightly kissed his lips as she refastened her blouse.

"You didn't tell me very much about your divorce," he said.

"But I did," she assured him. "I told you almost everything."

He frowned. "Was I a good listener?"

"The very best," she said, with a warm smile. "You made me feel desirable when I was convinced no man would ever want me again."

Jack closed his eyes as if attempting to fathom such a thing. "He must have been crazy."

"I . . . can't answer that."

"Do you still hate him?"

She lowered her eyes, not wanting him to read what was going on inside her. She had thought she did. Now she wasn't so sure. "I don't know. For a long time, I pretended the divorce didn't matter. I told myself I was lucky to have learned the kind of husband he was before we had children.

"It's only been since I met you that I realized how deeply I'd buried myself in denial. The divorce hurt, Jack. It was the most painful experience of my life." She wrapped her arms around his neck. "Every time I think about Peter, I feel incredibly sad."

"That's a beginning," Jack said softly, rubbing his chin against the side of her face. "A very good beginning."

Six

"I'm so pleased we could meet," Sarah said when Lacey arrived at the seafood restaurant. Seagulls flew overhead, chasing crows. The crows retaliated, pursuing the gulls in a battle over fertile feeding territory. From their window seat, Lacey could watch a lazy harbor seal sunning himself on the long pier. The day was glorious, and she felt the beginnings of joy creep into her soul. It had been a long, dark period. Her life had been dry and barren since the day Peter announced he wanted a divorce.

"I wanted to talk to you about Jack," Sarah said, her gaze fixed on her menu.

This didn't surprise Lacey, and if the truth be known she'd agreed to have lunch with Sarah for the same reason. Her curiosity about Jack was keen. He was an attractive, successful banker.

They were about the same age, she guessed, and she couldn't help wondering how he'd gotten to the ripe old age of thirty-three without being married.

"I understand you and Jack are seeing each other quite a bit these days."

Lacey didn't know why the truth unsettled her so, but she found herself fiddling with her napkin, bunching it in her hands. "He comes over to visit Cleo."

Sarah's soft laugh revealed her amusement. "It isn't Cleo who interests him, and we both know it. He's had his eye on you for over a year. The problem is, my dear brother doesn't know how to be subtle."

Lacey disagreed. "He's been more than patient."

"True," Sarah agreed reluctantly. "He didn't want to scare you off. We talked about you several times. He wanted my advice. I was the one who suggested he send you flowers. He was downright discouraged when you repeatedly turned him down. Who would have thought that silly tomcat would be the thing to bring you two together?"

Lacey smoothed the linen napkin across her lap. The time for being coy had long since passed. "I like your brother very much."

"He's wonderful." Once again Sarah admitted this with reluctance. "He liked you from the moment he first saw you."

"But why?" When Lacey moved into the apartment building she'd been an emotional wreck. The divorce had been less than a month old. She hadn't realized it at the time, but she'd been one of the walking wounded.

Sarah's look was knowing. "Jack's like that. He knew you'd been badly hurt and that you needed someone, the same way Dog did. He found Dog in a back alley, half starved and so mad he wouldn't let anyone near him. It took several weeks before Dog recognized Jack as a friend." She paused, leaned forward, and braced her elbows against the table. "But Jack was patient. He's been patient with you too, and it's paid off. I can't remember the last time he was so happy."

"I'm not a stray cat," Lacey said defensively. She wasn't keen on the comparison, but the similarity didn't escape her.

"Oh, no," Sarah said quickly. "I didn't mean to imply that. Jack would have my head for even suggesting such a thing. But you were hurting and Jack recognized it. If you want the truth, I think Jack should have been a doctor. It's just part of his nature to want to help others."

"I see." Lacey wasn't finding this conversation the least bit complimentary, but she couldn't deny what Sarah said. For the last year she'd been walking around in a shell. Only when Jack came into her life did she understand how important it was to deal with her divorce.

Sarah sighed and set the menu aside. "Jack's wonderful. That's why it's hard to understand why he's so unreasonable about me and Mark."

"I've never known Jack to be unreasonable."

"But he is," Sarah said, keeping her head lowered as if she was close to tears. "I love Mark; we want to be married someday. We just can't marry now, for a number of reasons. Sometimes I think Jack hates him."

"I'm sure that's not true." Lacey couldn't imagine Jack hating anyone, but she could easily understand his being overprotective.

"It's true," Sarah said heatedly. "Jack refuses to have anything to do with Mark, and do you know why?" Lacey wasn't given the opportunity to answer. "Because Jack thinks Mark's using me. Nothing I can say will convince him otherwise. It's the most ridiculous thing I've ever heard, and it's all because we're living together. As far as I can see, my brother needs to wake up and smell the coffee."

The waiter arrived with glasses of ice water and a basket filled with warm sourdough bread. Lacey smiled her appreciation, grateful for the interruption. The aroma of fresh bread was heavenly, but the conversation was becoming uncomfortable. She was not sure how to reply to Sarah. She was far more at ease having Sarah answer her questions about Jack than play-ing go-between for brother and sis-ter. Jack might be overprotective, but she couldn't imagine his disliking Mark without cause.

"What I'd really like is for you to talk to Jack for me," Sarah said, her eyes wide and pleading. "He'll listen to you, because—"

"I can't do that, Sarah," Lacey inter-rupted.

"I was hoping you'd consider it. I thought if you met Mark yourself, you'd be able to see how marvelous he is, and then you could tell Jack. You don't mind if he joins us, do you?"

Once again, Lacey wasn't given an opportunity to choose one way or the other. Sarah half rose from her seat and waved.

A sophisticated young man moved away from the bar and walked toward them, carrying his drink. Lacey studied Mark, trying to keep an open mind. As far as looks went, he was an attrac-tive man. He kissed Sarah's cheek, but his gaze moved smoothly to Lacey and lingered approvingly. They exchanged brief handshakes while Sarah made the introductions.

"I hope you don't mind if I join you," Mark said, pulling out a chair, "although every man here will think I'm greedy to be dining with the two most beautiful women in the room."

Mark didn't need to say another word for Lacey to understand Jack's disapproval. He was much too smooth. And she didn't like the way he looked at her—with a little too much curiosity. What she didn't understand was how Sarah could be so blind.

"Sarah and I are in a bit of a quandary." Mark reached for Sarah's hand and gripped it in his own.

"We need help in dealing with Jack," Sarah elaborated. "Mark suggested the two of us get together and talk to you about our problem. I'm not sure it's wise, but Mark seems to think that you—"

"Right," Mark cut in. "I feel you might say something that would smooth the waters between Sarah and her brother for me."

"You want me to talk to Jack on your

behalf?" she asked. Apparently Mark had no qualms about having her do his speaking for him. What Sarah's lover failed to understand was that Jack would react negatively to such an arrangement. Whatever small respect he had for Mark would be wiped out.

"Just mention that you've met Mark," Sarah coaxed. "You don't need to make an issue of it. I'm sure he'd listen to you. You see, Jack's living in the Middle Ages. Mark thinks Jack is jealous. My brother and I used to be really close—there wasn't anything I couldn't tell him." A wistful look clouded her pretty features. "It isn't like that anymore. It hurts, the way we argue. I can't help agreeing that it seems like jealousy."

Lacey wondered if that could possibly be true. "Jack's met Mark?"

"Oh, yes, plenty of times. From the very first, Jack's had a grudge against him."

"We started off on the wrong foot," Mark admitted dryly.

"What happened?" Lacey asked.

"Nothing," Sarah said defensively. "Absolutely nothing. But I've never been serious about anyone before, and Jack just can't deal with it."

Lacey didn't want to take sides, but she found herself saying, "I don't know Jack all that well, but I can't see him as the jealous sort."

"I know, but you see, I'm crazy about Mark and Jack knows it, and the way Mark figures—and me too—my brother needs to accept the fact that his little sister is all grown up, and he refuses to do it." Absently, Sarah tore off a piece of bread and held it between her hands, as if she wasn't sure what to do with it. "Can you help us, Lacey?"

"I doubt it," she said, as forthrightly and honestly as she could.

"Jack would listen to you," Sarah said.

Lacey smiled softly at the fervor of Sarah's belief that she had any influence on her brother. "I'm only his next-door neighbor."

"That's where you're wrong," she said, her voice raised with the strength of her conviction. "Jack really likes you. More than anyone in a good long while."

Lacey wasn't sure of that either, but she let it pass. "You want me to tell your brother that you're a mature woman capable of making her own decisions, whether he agrees with them or not."

"Exactly," Sarah said.

"That's what he needs to hear," Mark concurred.

"As an adult, you're free to love whomever you wish," Lacey said.

"Right again." Sarah's voice raised with the fervor of her conviction.

Mark smiled at Sarah and she smiled back. "We know what we're doing, isn't that right, baby?"

"I'm over twenty-one," Sarah announced.

"You're both competent judges of character," Lacey said.

"Of course." Sarah's grin widened. "I couldn't have said it better myself."

They were momentarily interrupted by the waiter, who returned for their order.

"Jack's not an unreasonable person," Lacey continued. "If that's the way you both feel, you don't need me to tell him. Do it yourselves, together."

"He won't listen," Sarah protested.

"Have you tried?"

Mark tore the roll in half and lowered his gaze. "Not exactly, but then it isn't like we've had much of an opportunity."

"Is it your living arrangement that's troubling Jack?" Lacey asked.

"That isn't permanent," Sarah told her.

"We'll be married someday," Mark said. "But not right away. We want to be married on our terms and not have them dictated by an older brother."

Lacey kept silent because she feared her own views on the subject wouldn't be welcome. Over the years several of her friends had opted for live-in arrangements. It might have been the luck of the draw, but they'd all come out of the relationships with regrets.

"Loving Mark isn't a mistake," Sarah insisted a bit too strongly. "We're perfect together."

The waiter delivered their salads, but by then Lacey had lost her appetite.

"And Sarah's perfect for me," Mark added, before reaching for his fork and digging into the plump shrimp that decorated the top of his huge salad.

"Mark loves me, and I love him," Sarah concluded. "As far as I'm concerned that's the most important thing."

Lacey saw that both Sarah and Mark felt they could change her mind. It was important to clear that up immediately. "I hope you can appreciate why I can't speak to Jack on your behalf."

"Yes," Sarah said sadly. "I just wish Jack wasn't so openly hostile."

"Sarah?" The husky male voice came from behind her. "Lacey? What are you two doing here?"

It was Jack.

Seven

"Hello, Jack," Sarah said, recovering first. She didn't look pleased. Lacey knew their relationship was strained and wished she could help, but she couldn't think of a way to lessen the tension between them. Jack ignored Mark completely. But then Mark didn't acknowledge him either.

"How are my two best girls?" Jack asked, disregarding Sarah's cool welcome. He slid out a chair and sat down without waiting for an invitation.

"Feel free to join us," Sarah muttered sarcastically.

"Hello, Jack," Lacey said, her heart reacting in a happy way despite Sarah and Mark's sour reception. She lowered her gaze abruptly when he focused his eyes on her. She didn't have any reason to feel guilty, but she did—a little.

It wasn't like she was doing something behind his back.

"Lacey and I were just having a little chat," Sarah said, after an awkward moment. "That's what you want to know, isn't it?"

"I didn't ask, Sarah. What you and Lacey talk about is none of my business." Jack ordered a cup of coffee and turned toward Lacey and Sarah, presenting Mark with a view of his back.

"If you must know, we discussed Mark and me," Sarah said, far more defensively than necessary.

Jack sipped his coffee, giving no outward indication that the topic of conversation troubled him. "Let's change the subject, shall we?"

"I bet you were hoping Lacey would talk some sense into me," Sarah said stiffly. "Well, you're wrong."

Jack leveled his gaze on his sister, his look wide and disapproving.

"You don't need to worry," Sarah continued on the same touchy note. "Lacey has refused to talk to you on our behalf."

"Mark asked her to?"

"Of course," Sarah returned belligerently. "What else can he do since you flatly refuse to speak to him?"

"I don't appreciate your dragging Lacey into this," Jack said, not bothering to hide his disapproval.

"You don't need to worry," Sarah snapped back. "It won't happen again."

It upset Lacey to watch the two of them bicker, knowing how deeply they cared for each other. But she was helpless to do anything more than listen.

"How's Cleo?" Jack looked at Lacey in a clear effort to find a more pleasant topic.

Lacey reached for her coffee. "Getting fat."

"Good," he said absently.

"How can you ignore Mark like this?" Sarah demanded. "You act as if he isn't even here."

Jack remained stubbornly silent for a moment before asking, "Have you ever asked Mark why I behave toward him the way I do?" He sipped his coffee. "It would be very interesting if he admitted the truth."

"Let's get out of here." Mark stood abruptly and reached for Sarah's hand. "We don't need him, Sarah, we never have. Let's just leave well enough alone."

"But, Mark—" Sarah looked from her lover to her brother, her eyes bright with indecision.

"Are you coming or not?" Mark demanded irritably, dropping her hand.

"You could try talking to Jack," Sarah suggested on a tentative note, sounding unsure and pitiful. Lacey's heart went out to her.

"Do what you want." Mark turned and started to walk away.

Sarah vacillated, torn with indecision, before sighing heavily. "Mark, wait," she called, obediently trotting after him.

The silence that followed Sarah's departure was heavy with tension. Jack's face darkened with what appeared to be regret before he looked once more to Lacey. It seemed, for an awkward moment, that he had forgotten she was there.

"Jack," she said softly, touching his hand.

"I'm sorry." He shook his head as if to clear it. "I hope Sarah and Mark didn't make pests of themselves."

"Not in the least," Lacey assured him. "She's a delightful young woman, if a bit confused." Although it wasn't any of Lacey's business, she wanted to know. "Why do you actively dislike Mark?"

"There are several reasons," he said pointedly, "but you don't need to worry about me and my sister. It's not your affair."

"I see," she answered. She couldn't help feeling hurt by his abrupt dismissal. "I shouldn't have asked."

Jack sighed. "I saw him with another girl soon after Sarah moved in with him. It was clear they were more than casual acquaintances, but when I mentioned it to Sarah she claimed I was lying in an effort to break them up. Naturally Mark denied everything. It's like my beautiful, intelligent sister has been hypnotized. She can't seem to see what's right under her nose."

"It's probably the most difficult thing you can do, isn't it?"

"What?" Jack wanted to know.

Lacey gently squeezed his hand. "Watch her make a mistake and know there's no way to keep her from making it."

Jack studied her for a long moment and nodded. "It's hell. And the worst part is losing the closeness we once shared. I don't know how she can be so blind."

"Sarah can't see what she doesn't want to see." It had been the same way with Lacey. The evidence was there, but she'd refused to notice what was apparent to everyone else.

❖   ❖   ❖

When Lacey returned to the office, her head was filled with Jack and his sister. She wished there were some way she could help but knew it was impossible.

Mr. Sullivan was waiting for her, impatiently pacing the cramped quarters. As she stepped inside, he glanced pointedly at his watch.

"You're late," he announced.

"Five minutes," she said calmly, sitting down at her desk. After all the times she'd come in early and stayed late, she certainly didn't feel guilty for going five minutes over her lunch hour.

"Were you aware Mrs. Baxter was due this afternoon to go over wallpaper samples?" he asked, with thinly disguised irritation.

"Yes," Lacey answered, not understanding why her employer was so flustered.

"Well, Mrs. Baxter was in town earlier than she anticipated and stopped in. You weren't here." Accusation rang in his voice as clear as church bells. "I was left to deal with her myself, and I don't mind telling you, Lacey, that woman unnerves me. You should have been here."

Lacey straightened in her chair, unwilling to accept his censure. "Mr. Sullivan," she said evenly, refusing to allow him to badger her, "I'm entitled to my lunch hour."

He pressed his lips together and walked over to his own desk. "You're the wallpaper expert," he returned flippantly.

"I am?" If he felt that way, he should pay her accordingly. There would never be a better time to point this out.

"Of course you are," he snapped. "Whenever customers are interested in wallpaper I refer them to you."

"How nice," Lacey said.

He was making this almost easy for her. To her surprise, she wasn't the least bit nervous.

"How long have I worked for you now, Mr. Sullivan?"

"Ah . . ." He picked up a pencil and figured some numbers on a pad as if her question required several algebraic calculations. "It must be a year or more."

"Exactly a year. Do you recall that when you hired me we made an agreement?"

"Yes, of course." He stiffened as if he knew what was coming.

"There was to be a salary evaluation after six months and another at one year. The months have slipped by, and I've taken on a good deal of the responsibility of running the business for you, and now you tell me I'm your wallpaper expert! I can assure you no *expert* makes the low wages I do. I believe, Mr. Sullivan, that you owe me a substantial raise, possibly two." Having said all this in one giant breath, she was winded when she finished.

She'd done it! After all the weeks of moaning and groaning, of complaining and berating herself, she'd actually asked for the raise she deserved. It hadn't even been hard! She watched her employer and waited for his response.

"I owe you a raise?" Mr. Sullivan sounded shocked, as if the thought had never occurred to him. "I'll have to check my records. You might very well be right. I'll look into it and get back to you first thing in the morning." Having said that, Mr. Sullivan promptly disappeared—something he was doing more frequently of late, leaving her with the burden of dealing with everything herself.

Lacey felt as though a great weight

had been lifted from her shoulders. It was as if whatever had bound her had fallen away.

❧   ❧   ❧

The first person she sought out that afternoon was Jack. She went directly from the elevator to his apartment, knocking several times, eager to share her news. To her disappointment, he wasn't home. She realized how important he'd become to her. It was as if none of this were real until she'd shared it with her neighbor.

Letting herself inside her own apartment, she promptly greeted Cleo and then reached for the phone. Jeanne answered on the second ring.

"I asked Mr. Sullivan for a raise," she said without so much as a hello. "Jeanne, I'm so happy, I could cry. It just happened. He made some offhand comment about me being his wallpaper expert, and I said if that was the case I should be properly compensated."

"That's great, and about time too, girl. Congratulations!"

Lacey knew Jeanne would be pleased for her, if for nothing more than garnering the courage to ask.

"I owe you so much," Lacey said, the emotion bubbling in her voice. "I really do. Not long ago you claimed if I wanted to be a victim, you couldn't help me, and I realized you were right. And Jack too, he's been—" She stopped, thinking how much Jack had helped her. Not in the same way as Jeanne, but by his own gentle understanding, he'd encouraged her and helped her to find herself. She understood for the first time how confronting Mr. Sullivan was tied in with her divorce. She'd come out of her marriage emotionally crippled, carrying a load of grief and insecurity that had burdened her whole life.

"You haven't mentioned Jack much lately," Jeanne commented. "How's it going with you two?"

"I haven't talked about Jack?" Lacey hedged. "It's going fine, just fine."

"*Fine* suggests it's going great."

Cleo wove her way around Lacey's

feet, demanding attention. With the tip of her shoe, Lacey booted the catnip toy as a distraction. Cleo raced after it.

"Now," Jeanne said, heaving a giant breath, "tell me how much of a raise Mr. Sullivan's giving you."

"He didn't say . . . exactly. All he said was that he was going to think about it overnight."

"Don't let him weasel out of it," Jeanne warned.

"Don't worry," Lacey said. "He wouldn't dare." At the moment she felt invincible, capable of dealing with anything or anyone.

As soon as she was off the phone, Lacey gave Cleo the attention she demanded. "How are you doing, girl?" Lacey asked. "I bet you're anxious to have those kittens." She stroked her back and Cleo purred contentedly. "Jack and I will find good homes for your babies," Lacey assured her. "You don't have a thing to worry about."

Jack didn't get home until after six. The minute she heard movement on the other side of her kitchen wall, she hurried over to his apartment. She tapped out a staccato knock against his door and was cheered to hear him humming on the other side.

"Who is it?" he called out.

"Lacey."

The door flew open. The minute he appeared, she vaulted into his arms, spreading kisses over his face. He blinked as if he wasn't sure what was happening.

"Lacey?" His eyes were wide with surprise and delight. "What was that for?"

"A thank-you." She wove her arms around his neck and kissed him again. "I'm so happy."

"My guess is something happened after we met at lunch."

She rewarded his genius, taking more time, savoring the kiss. With every beat of her heart, she thanked God for sending Jack into her lonely, bleak life.

"I'm almost afraid to ask what this is all about. Whatever it is, don't let me stop you." He closed the door with his foot and carried her into the living room.

She hugged him tight. His shirt was unfastened. Either he was dressing or undressing, she couldn't tell which. Her trembling body moved against his.

"Are you going to tell me what we're celebrating?" he asked her breathlessly.

"A raise," she said. "And long overdue. You see, I had to ask for it, and doing that was a growing experience for me." She paused to rub her nose against his. "I realize this probably sounds silly, but I couldn't make myself ask, and it got to be this really big thing, like a monster, and then I was terrified."

"But you did it?"

"Yes. I owe it all to you—and to my friend Jeanne. Knowing you has helped me so much, Jack. You've given me my confidence back. I'm not sure how you managed it, but since we've been . . . neighborly, it seems everything's turned around for me."

"I couldn't be more pleased, and

naturally I'll accept the credit," he said warmly.

"Mr. Sullivan's going to think about it overnight, but you see this isn't about the money. It's about me."

"You certainly didn't have any problem confronting me when Dog stole Cleo's virginity. As I recall you were ready with a tidy list of demands."

"That was different. I wasn't the one affected, it was Cleo. I didn't have the least bit of trouble sticking up for my cat."

"I'd like to complain, but I won't," Jack said. "I'm more than pleased that Dog decided to call upon Cleo; otherwise I don't know how long it would have taken me to break through those barriers of yours."

He kissed her then, slowly, thoroughly, leaving her trembling when he'd finished.

"We'll celebrate. Dinner, dancing, a night on the town. We'll—" He stopped abruptly and closed his eyes.

"What?"

"I've got another one of those stupid dinner meetings this evening."

"It doesn't matter." She was disappointed, but she understood. "This is rather short notice. We'll celebrate another time. It doesn't matter, truly it doesn't." Nothing could mar her happiness. "How soon do you have to leave?"

He glanced at his watch and frowned. "Ten minutes."

"I'd better go."

"No." He kissed her hungrily.

"Jack"—she managed a protest, weak at best—"you'll be late for your dinner."

"Yeah, I know."

"Jack!"

He kissed her nose. "Spoilsport. Remember, we're on for dinner on the town tomorrow night."

"I'll remember."

Lacey returned to her apartment in a daze. When she slumped onto the sofa, Cleo settled in her lap, and she slowly stroked the cat's back, thinking over her day. Lacey wasn't sure how long she sat there before someone knocked on her door. Checking the peephole, Lacey was shocked to see who it was.

"Sarah!" she said, unlocking her door.

Jack's sister took one look at her and burst into tears. "Oh, Lacey, I've been such a fool!"

Eight

"Sarah, what happened?" Lacey led Jack's sister into her apartment. Sarah slumped onto the love seat and covered her face with both hands. Several seconds passed before she was able to speak.

"I . . . found out Mark's involved with someone else. I found them together, in our bed. I thought I was going to be sick . . . I couldn't believe my own eyes. How could I have been so stupid?"

"Oh, Sarah!" Lacey wrapped her arm around Sarah's shoulders. "I'm so sorry."

"Jack *told* me Mark was seeing someone else, but I didn't believe him. I loved Mark . . . I really loved him. How could I have been so stupid?" She buried her face in Lacey's shoulder.

The experience was nearly a mirror image of her own, so Lacey could appreciate the devastating sense of betrayal Sarah was feeling.

"I know what you're going through," Lacey said when Sarah's sobbing had slowed. She brought her a hot cup of tea with plenty of sugar to help ward off the shock.

"How could you?" Sarah said. She looked up at Lacey, her face devoid of makeup, her eyes filled with a hollow, familiar pain. The afghan Lacey's mother had crocheted for a Christmas present was wrapped over the younger woman's shoulders as if she'd been chilled to the bone. Sarah looked as if she were six years old.

"It's like your whole world has been violently turned upside down. But it's much more than that. The sense of betrayal is the worst emotional pain there is."

"You too?"

Lacey nodded. "My husband—ex-husband, now—left me for another woman. Apparently they'd been lovers for months, but I didn't have a clue. When Peter asked for a divorce, I thought I'd die." Memories of that final confrontation filtered through Lacey's mind. She found, somewhat to her surprise, that although they saddened her, she didn't feel the crushing agony that had been with her for the last year and a half.

"What . . . what did you do afterward?"

Lacey reached for Sarah's hand and squeezed her fingers. "After the divorce was final, I packed everything I owned and moved to San Francisco."

"Then it must not have been very long ago."

"The divorce was final last year about this time."

Sarah sipped her tea. "I was blind to what was happening. I trusted Mark, really trusted him. I nearly allowed him to destroy my love for my brother."

"Don't blame yourself."

"But I do!" Sarah cried. "Looking back, I can't believe I sided against Jack. He's never lied to me, and yet I believed everything Mark was telling me about my brother being jealous and all that other garbage."

"I believed too," Lacey said, "but when you love someone, the trust is automatic. Why should we suspect a man of cheating when such behavior would never occur to us? The very thought of being unfaithful to Peter was repugnant to me."

Sarah cradled the mug between her palms. "Do you think you'll ever be able to trust a man again?"

"Yes," Lacey answered, after some length, "but not in the same blind way. I couldn't bear to live my life being constantly suspicious. The burden of that would ruin any future relationships. I'm not the same woman I was eighteen months ago. Peter's betrayal has marked me forever." She hesitated, unsure of how much she should admit about the changes knowing Jack had brought into her life. "It wasn't until recently that I felt I could say this, but I believe it changed me for the better."

"How do you mean?"

"It was a long, painful ordeal. Only in the last month have I come to terms with what happened. For a long time I thought I hated Peter, but that wasn't true. How could I hate him when I'd never stopped loving him?"

"What do you feel for him now?"

Lacey had to think over the question. "Mostly I don't feel anything. I've forgiven him."

"You? He should be the one to beg *your* forgiveness."

Lacey smiled, knowing Peter as she did. "I could wait until hell freezes over, and that would never happen. Peter believes *I* was the one who failed *him*, and perhaps I did in some way. He needed an excuse to rationalize what he was doing."

"Mark blamed me too. How could you forgive Peter? I don't understand."

"You'd be right to say he didn't ask for my forgiveness. But I didn't do it for *him*, I did it for *me*. Otherwise his betrayal would have destroyed me."

"I still don't understand."

"In the beginning," Lacey said, "I couldn't deal with the pain so I pretended I wasn't hurt. But in the last month, I've realized that I needed to let go of Peter and the failed marriage, and the only way to do it was to admit my own faults and forgive him. If I didn't, I might never have let go of my bitterness."

Fresh tears brimmed in Sarah's eyes. "I'll never be as wise as you are."

Lacey laughed. "Oh, Sarah, if only you knew how very long it took me to reconcile myself to this divorce. I have Jack to thank, and my friend Jeanne. Even Cleo played a role."

"Jack's wonderful," Sarah admitted and bit her lower lip. "I've treated him abominably."

"That's one thing about brothers, they're forgiving. At least we can trust that Jack is. He's a special man, Sarah, and I can't believe you'll have any more problems setting matters straight with him."

They sat and talked, and as the hours passed Lacey realized how much they had in common. It was nearly ten o'clock when the doorbell chimed. The two women looked at each other.

"You don't need to worry. I'm sure it's not Mark."

Lacey checked the peephole anyway. It was Jack. Unlatching the chain, she opened the door and was immediately brought into his arms. He kissed her as if it had been weeks instead of hours since they'd last seen each other.

"Jack." Sarah's voice cut into the sensual fog that surrounded Lacey.

Jack abruptly broke off the kiss but kept his arm around Lacey's waist. She watched his face as he discovered his sister sitting on the sofa, wrapped in Lacey's afghan. His gaze went from Sarah to Lacey and then back again.

"Sit down," Lacey said, easing her way out of his embrace. "Sarah has something to tell you." Then, because she knew how difficult it would be, she leaned close and whispered, "Be gentle with her."

❈   ❈   ❈

"Lacey," Jack said irritably, "don't lift that, it's too heavy for you."

"I'm fine," she insisted, hauling the carton out of the back of the rented van. It was heavy, but nothing she couldn't handle. Sarah had found an apartment of her own, and Jack and Lacey were helping her move. It had been an eventful month. Sarah had temporarily moved in with Lacey and the two women had talked, often long into the night.

"That should do it," Sarah said, as Lacey set the carton on the kitchen countertop. She looked past Lacey and whispered, "What's wrong with Jack? He's been a real crab all morning, and he wasn't much better last night, either. Did you notice?"

Lacey had, but she hadn't wanted to say anything. "I don't know what's wrong." But something was.

"If anyone can get it out of him, it's you."

Lacey wondered if that was true. After the last month she felt as close to Sarah as if they were really sisters. And in that time she'd come to another, more profound realization.

She was deeply in love with Jack.

For someone who was convinced she was constitutionally incapable of falling in love again, this was big news.

"I can't thank you two enough,"

Sarah said when Jack returned from the truck. "I don't know what I would have done these last weeks without you." She hugged them, then turned away in an effort to hide the tears that glistened in her dark eyes. "I'll be fine now. You two go and have fun. I don't want you to worry about me."

Jack hesitated. "You're sure?"

"Positive." Sarah made busywork around her compact kitchen, removing several items from the closest box and setting them on the counter. All the while her back was to them. "Please," she added.

Remembering her own experience, Lacey whispered, "She'll be fine. All she needs is time."

Together Lacey and Jack walked outside to where Jack had parked the moving van. He opened the passenger door and helped her inside.

Lacey removed her bandanna and shook her head to free the thick strands of dark hair that were plastered against her face. Jack climbed into the driver's seat. She noticed how his hands tightened around the steering wheel. For several seconds he just sat there. Then he started the engine and moved out into traffic. But he still seemed deep in thought. Something was wrong.

"Jack," she said softly, "what's troubling you?"

Her voice broke him out of his reverie, and he smiled as if he hadn't a care in the world. "Not a thing. How about sharing a hot fudge sundae with me after we take the truck back?"

It sounded wonderful, but Lacey had discovered in the last few weeks that almost every minute she spent in Jack's company was special. *He* was special.

"Are you worried about Sarah?" Lacey pried gently, wondering at his somber mood. Something was on his mind, but she couldn't force him to tell her. He would speak up when he was ready, she decided.

"Not as much now as when she was living with Mark. Although it's been hard on her, discovering exactly what kind of man he is was the best thing that could have happened."

"She'll be fine," Lacey said confidently.

"Thanks to you."

"Oh, hardly. Sarah will come away from this experience a little more mature and a whole lot smarter. I know I did with Peter. But it takes time. Rome wasn't built in a day."

"I'll say. Look how long it took me to get to know you."

"It was worth the effort, wasn't it?"

He took one hand from the wheel and patted her knee. They were sitting so close to each other that their hips touched. The morning was muggy, but neither of them moved, enjoying this small intimacy. "The wait was well worth the while," he agreed and then added, his eyes dark and serious, "I'm crazy about you, Lacey; I have been for months."

"I'm crazy about you too," she returned softly.

What was definitely crazy was that they should admit their feelings for each other in a moving van in the heavy flow of San Francisco traffic.

After having spoken so freely, both

seemed a little embarrassed, a little re-
lieved, and a whole lot in love. Lacey
felt as if she were in college all over
again. The years of her marriage and
the aftermath of the divorce vanished,
as if they'd never happened.

Leaving his car in the underground
parking lot, they caught the elevator.
The instant the door slid closed, Lacey
was in Jack's arms. His mouth sought
hers with the desperation of a man
locked in a dark room, unable to find
the exit. His arms half lifted her from
the floor, giving her the perfect excuse
to cling to him.

"I'm crazy about you," she said. She
felt drunk, as if she'd spent the last few
hours sitting in a bar instead of the last
few moments in his arms.

He caught her face between his
hands and kissed her until she trembled and whimpered. He moaned.

"Jack." From somewhere deep inside she managed a weak protest.
"We're still in the elevator."

He lifted his head and looked around.
"We are?"

She wrapped her arms around his

waist and tilted back her head to smile up at him.

"Where's your sense of adventure?" he teased, kissing her nose. He reached over and pushed the button for the fourth floor.

This intense feeling of desire was new to her. If he didn't continue kissing her, loving her, touching her, Lacey thought she'd die. It was as if years of dammed-up longing had broken free deep inside of her, swamping her senses.

He kissed her again and she sagged against him just as the elevator delivered them to the fourth floor.

"Your place or mine?" he asked, and then made the decision for her. "Yours."

Her hand trembled when she gave him her keys, and she was gratified to see his fingers weren't any steadier. In that moment, she loved him so much she couldn't bear it a second longer. Her arms circled his middle and she kissed the underside of his jaw, teasing him with her tongue, running it down his neck to the hollow at the base of his throat and sucking gently.

"Lacey, stop," he protested.

"Do you mean that?" she whispered, lifting her face.

"No . . . never stop loving me." The door opened and they all but stumbled inside.

It was then she heard Cleo's pitiful meow. Jack heard it too. He glanced over his shoulder and then turned his gaze back to her. His eyes were tightly shut.

"Cleo's having her kittens," he announced and moved away from her.

Nine

"Cleo's having her kittens now!"

Lacey hurried into the apartment.

"Oh, my goodness!" She pressed her hands over her mouth and stared into the closet, where Cleo had made herself a comfortable bed in a darkened corner.

The Abyssinian meowed pitifully.

"Oh, Cleo," Lacey whispered.

Cleo ignored her, rose from her nest, and walked over to Jack, weaving between his legs, her long tail sliding around his calf. Then moved back into the closet and cried again, softly, pleadingly.

"She seems to want you," Lacey murmured, unable to disguise her amazement. It didn't make sense that Cleo would be more comfortable with

Jack. After all, Lacey was the one who fed and nurtured her.

"She wants *me*?"

"It wasn't me she was crying for just now." Didn't anyone understand the meaning of commitment anymore? Lacey wondered. Even her cat turned to someone else in her moment of need.

Cleo was up again, seeking Jack's attention. He squatted down in front of the open closet door and patted her gently while whispering reassurances.

"Should I boil water or something?" Lacey asked anxiously. The moment had finally arrived, but she hadn't a clue as to what her role should be. She'd assumed Cleo would calmly give birth to her kittens one day while Lacey was at work.

"Boil water?" Jack asked. "Whatever for?"

"I . . . don't know. Coffee, I guess." She paced the carpet behind Jack in short, quick steps. Seconds earlier they'd been wrapped in an impassioned embrace, and now lovemaking was the furthest thing from either of their minds.

"How's she doing?" Lacey asked, peeking over his shoulder.

"Great, so far. It looks as if the first kitten is about to be born."

"How's Cleo?" Lacey asked again, her fingertips pressed against her lips. "Is she afraid? I don't think I can bear to see her in pain."

Jack looked up at Lacey, reached for her hand, and kissed her knuckles. "She's fine. Stop worrying or you'll make yourself ill."

No sooner had he said the words than Lacey's stomach cramped. She wrapped her hands around her waist, sank onto the end of the mattress, and leaned forward. "Jack, I don't feel so good."

"Go make that coffee you were talking about earlier," he suggested. "At this point Cleo's doing better than you are."

Cleo cried out and Jack turned his attention back to the closet.

"She just delivered the first kitten," he announced, his pleasure keen. "Good

girl, Cleo," he said excitedly. "My goodness, will you look at that! Cleo's kitten
is the spitting image of Dog."

Lacey hurried off the bed to look.
Her stomach didn't feel much better,
but she understood the source of her
discomfort. She was experiencing sympathetic labor pains. "He does look like
Dog." She squatted down next to Jack
and studied the ugly little creature. "I
don't mind telling you, Jack, this unnerves me."

"I could go for a cup of coffee," he
said. "Cleo and I are doing fine."

Lacey hurried into the kitchen. Once
she was there, she decided there was
no need to rush. As Jack had so elo-
quently told her, he had everything under control.

"How's it going?" she asked when
she returned with their coffee.

"Great. I think Cleo's just about ready
to deliver a second kitten."

Lacey wasn't interested in viewing
the birthing process, so she sat on the
bed and let Jack play midwife.

"Here it comes," he said after a few
minutes, his voice elevated with excite-

ment. "This one's just like Dog too." He turned with a proud smile as if he'd given birth himself.

Grumbling, Lacey sank onto the carpet next to Jack. Cleo was busy licking off her tiny offspring. As far as Lacey could tell the kittens were no bigger than fur balls and ugly as sin, but that didn't keep her heart from swelling with a flood of emotions.

"Do you think she's finished?"

"I don't know," Jack returned. "How long do these things usually take?"

Lacey laughed. "How would I know?"

"You intended to breed her, didn't you?"

"Yes, before Dog so rudely interrupted my plans."

Jack wiggled his eyebrows. "You're pleased he did, aren't you?"

Lacey wasn't willing to admit anything of the sort. "You'll note that once Dog had his fun with Cleo, he was on his merry way."

"Perhaps, but with Cleo having Dog's family—well, it sort of cemented our relationship, don't you think?"

She suppressed a smile. "I guess it did."

"You can breed her next time if you're really serious about it."

He was right; it would be foolish to claim otherwise. "I'll get the pamphlet Dr. Christman gave me. That should tell us how long this process takes." She left him momentarily and returned reading the material the vet had given her.

"I think Cleo might be finished," Jack announced when Lacey walked into the bedroom and sat on the end of the mattress. "She's lavishing attention on her kittens and not acting the way she was earlier."

"It says here the birthing process generally takes a couple of hours," she recited and glanced at her watch. It hadn't taken nearly that amount of time for Cleo.

Before she could say as much, Jack said, "We don't have any idea how long she was in labor before we arrived."

"Right. It could easily have been two hours." She felt a tremendous sense of relief that it was over. "She only had two kittens, but it says right here that Abyssinians generally have smaller litters and Siamese have larger ones. That's interesting."

"I guess we should thank our lucky stars Cleo only has the two."

"Speaking of which," Lacey said righteously, "you never gave me the name of the family taking your half of the litter."

"I'll give one to Sarah," Jack said confidently. "A pet will do her good. Besides, she owes me big-time."

"But does Sarah want a cat?" Lacey might think of Jack's sister as family, but she didn't want to foist an animal off on her if Sarah wasn't willing.

"Of course she wants one. Dog and Cleo's offspring are special. Besides, a kitten will keep her company while she gets over Mark." He frowned as if he found speaking the other man's name repulsive. "It shouldn't take long for her to forget that rat."

"Don't be so sure," Lacey told him. "I was married to a man who displayed many of the same characteristics. Be patient with her," she advised again, and then added with a gentle smile, "As patient as you were with me."

"You've spoken so little of your marriage."

"If you review what happened with Sarah and change the names in the appropriate places, the story's the same, with only a few differences," she amended. "The biggest difference is that I was married to Peter. A couple of months after I moved here, I heard from a well-meaning friend who thought I should know that he'd married his blond cupcake and they were expecting a baby."

"Some friend."

Her smile was sad. "That's what I thought. The news devastated me. Not because he'd remarried, but because he'd been adamant about us not having children when I wanted a family so badly."

Jack drank from his coffee and seemed to be mulling over the information. "You're over him now?"

Lacey wasn't entirely sure how to answer him. Her hesitation appeared to give Jack some concern. He leveled his gaze at her and frowned darkly.

"Yes, I'm over him, and no, I'm not."

The corner of Jack's mouth jerked upward. "That's about as clear as swamp water."

"I don't love him anymore, if that's what you're asking. The hardest part was having to let go of the dream of what our lives could have been like together."

"Have you?" The words were stark and issued without emotion.

"Yes." She wanted to thank him for the large part he'd played in the healing process, but he didn't seem receptive to it. Although he'd asked her about Peter and her marriage, he seemed to find it uncomfortable to listen to the sorry details of her life with her ex-husband.

Jack stood and wandered into the living room, taking his coffee with him. When she joined him, she found him standing in front of the small window that looked down over the street. He didn't turn around. It was almost as if he'd forgotten she was with him.

"Jack?"

He turned around and offered her a fleeting grin.

"Does it bother you to discuss my ex-husband?"

He shook his head, and set his mug aside. "Not in the least. I was the one who asked, remember?"

"Yes, but you seemed—I don't know, upset, I guess. Peter was a part of my life, an important part for several years.

"The divorce was difficult for me, but I learned from it. I matured. Blaming Peter isn't important any longer. I understand now that I played a part in the death of our marriage. I wasn't the perfect wife."

"You say you don't love him anymore?"

She gestured weakly. "Let me put it like this. I don't hate him. My happiness doesn't hinge on what's happening in his life. My happiness hinges on me and the choices I make, and I've decided to live a good life." She hoped it would be with Jack. With all her heart, she prayed he felt as strongly about her as she did him.

He smiled. Lacey swore she'd never seen anyone more beautiful. It was strange, she realized, to feel that way about a man. It wasn't so much his looks, although heaven knew he was handsome. What she found so appealing about Jack was who he was as a person. He was trustworthy and generous. He'd helped restore her faith in love and life. His love had been a precious gift for which she would always be thankful.

"Jack," she whispered, "what's wrong?" Something was still bothering him.

He walked over to Lacey and tenderly gathered her in his arms. He rested his chin against the top of her head, and she heard a sigh rumble through his chest.

"You got your raise from Mr. Sullivan?" he asked.

"Yes." Lacey was sure she'd told him, but they'd both been so wrapped up in helping Sarah that he must have forgotten. "A very healthy one."

"Good."

Lacey eased away from his chest

and met his gaze. "Why are you asking about Mr. Sullivan?"

"You love your job, don't you? Especially now that you're getting the respect and the money you deserve?"

"Yes, but what does that have to do with us?"

He brought her back into his embrace. "I love my job too. I've worked for California Fidelity for nearly ten years. Last Thursday I was given a promotion. This is something I've worked toward for years, but I never dreamed it would happen so quickly. It took me completely by surprise."

"Jack, that's wonderful." Stepping up on her tiptoes, she kissed him, so proud she felt she would burst. "Why didn't you say something sooner? We could have celebrated."

"My promotion means something else, Lacey."

"I'm sure you'll have added responsibilities. Oh, Jack, I couldn't be more pleased for you."

"It means," he said, cupping her shoulders, "I have to move."

The blood rushed out of her face so fast, Lacey felt faint. "Move? Where?"

He sighed and looked away from her. "Seattle."

Ten

"Seattle," Lacey echoed, stunned. "When did you intend to tell me, before or after you had your way with me?" Stepping away from him, she pushed the hair away from her head, leaving her hands there, elbows extended. "You're no better than Dog!"

"What's Dog got to do with this? You're being ridiculous."

"I'm not. You were going to make love to me and then casually mention you were being transferred?" It was all clear to her now. Rainwater clear. Just like the tomcat he called a pet, he was going to take what he wanted and walk out of her life.

"I didn't plan anything of the sort. You don't have any reason to be so angry. Besides, nothing happened."

"Thanks to Cleo. And for your information, I . . . have every right to be angry." Her fragile voice wobbled with emotion but gained strength with each word. "It'd be best if you left."

"Not until we've talked this out." He planted his feet as if to suggest a bulldozer wouldn't budge him before he was good and ready.

She pointed her index finger at him while she gathered her thoughts together, which unfortunately had scattered like water-starved cattle toward a river. "I've heard about men like you."

"What?" He stared at her as if he needed to examine her more closely. "Lacey, for the love of heaven, stop right now before you say something you'll regret."

"I most certainly will say something." She walked over to the door and held it open for him. "You . . . you can't drop a bombshell like that and expect me not to react. As for regrets, trust me, Jack Walker, I've got plenty of those. It'll take years to sort through them all."

"All right, all right." He raised his hands in surrender. Actually he posed as if she held a six-shooter on him.

"Please, close the door. Let's sit down and talk this over like two civilized people."

"Are you suggesting I'm not civilized? Because I'm telling you right now, I've had about as much as I can take."

"Sit down," he said calmly and gestured toward her sofa. "Please."

Lacey debated whether she should do as he asked or not. She crossed her arms under her breasts and glared at him. "I prefer to stand."

"Will you close the door?"

She hadn't realized her foot had continued to hold it open. "All right," she said stiffly, as if this were a large concession. Chin held high, she moved, and the door closed with a decidedly loud click.

"This is what I thought we'd do," Jack said, pacing in front of the window he'd been staring out only moments earlier.

"We?" she asked, wanting him to think she resented the way he automatically included her.

"Me," he amended, casting her a sour look. "I'm going to accept the promotion, Lacey. I thought about it long and hard, and I can't let this opportunity pass. The timing could be better, but I can't change that. I worked hard for this, and just because—"

"Of me?" she finished for him. "You don't need to worry, Jack, I wasn't going to ask you to turn down such a wonderful opportunity." Despite the shock and the betrayal she felt, maintaining her outrage was becoming difficult. Her voice softened considerably. "I wouldn't ever ask such a thing of you."

"I thought I could fly down for a weekend once a month," he suggested.

Once a month, she mused, her heart so heavy it felt as if it had dropped all the way to her knees. After having made such an issue of standing, she felt the sudden need to sit down.

Slumping onto the edge of the love seat, she bit her lower lip. So this was what was to become of them. Once-a-month dates. Lacey wasn't foolish enough to believe it would be otherwise. Long-distance relationships were difficult. They'd both start out with good intentions, but she noted he didn't say where these monthly meetings would lead.

Jack motioned with his hands. "Say something. Anything. I know it's not the ideal solution. It's going to be hard on me too."

"Expensive, too," she said. Already she could see the handwriting on the wall. He'd fly down for visits the first couple of months, and then he'd skip a month and she wouldn't hear from him the following one.

"We can make this work, Lacey."

Blinking back the tears, she stood and walked over to stand in front of him. His features blurred as her tears brimmed. She pressed her hands against the sides of his face, leaned forward, and kissed him. The electricity between them all but crackled, and it was several moments before Lacey found the strength and the courage to pull away.

"I . . . asked Sarah why you wanted to date me." She found it almost impossible to speak normally. "She told me you've been like this all your life. You find someone hurting and broken, someone in need of a little tenderness, and then you lavish them with love. What she didn't say was that once they were strong again, you'd step back and wish them a fond farewell."

Jack's brow condensed with a thick frown. "We aren't talking about the same thing. If you must know, you did represent a certain challenge from the moment we met. Until you, I'd never had much of a problem getting a woman to agree to go out with me. As for this other business, you're way off base."

"What about Dog?"

The frown darkened considerably. "What about him?"

"The lost and lonely alley cat you found and loved."

A hint of a smile touched his lips. "I don't think Dog would appreciate that description. We more or less tolerated each other in the beginning. These days, we share a tentative friendship."

"You took him in, gave him a home, and—"

"Hold on just one minute," Jack said sternly. "You're not suggesting that my friendship with Dog has anything to do with us, are you?"

It was apparent he didn't understand or appreciate the similarities. It would be one of the most difficult things she'd ever do to say good-bye to Jack, but despite what she'd claimed, she'd do it without regrets. He'd given her far more than he'd ever know. With Jack's love and support, she had learned to let go of the past. His love had given her the courage to move forward.

"Thank you," she whispered. She dropped her hands and stepped away.

"What are you thanking me for?" he demanded. "And why does it sound like another way of saying good-bye?"

She didn't so much as blink. "Because it is."

He paled visibly. "You don't mean that," he murmured.

Lacey couldn't think of anything more to say. Arguments crowded her mind. It would be easy to pretend that nothing would change after he moved to Seattle, but she knew it would.

Within a few months, Lacey would become little more than a memory of someone he once cared for. As he said, he didn't have a problem finding women interested in going out with him.

With all this talk of get-togethers, Lacey noticed, he wasn't offering her any promises. But to be fair, he hadn't sought any from her either.

"So it's over, just like that?" he said stiffly. "It was nice knowing you, have a good life, and all that rot?"

It sounded cold and crass, but basically he had it right. Unable to look him in the eye, Lacey nodded and lowered her head.

"In other words, once I walk out that door, that's it?"

"It's better this way," she whispered, the words barely making it past the lump in her throat. She prayed he'd leave before she disgraced herself further by weeping openly.

"Easier, in the long run. I'd rather end this now and be done with it. The woman I love is ordering me out of her life. It doesn't make sense."

"Exactly what are you offering me, Jack?" she asked defiantly. "A weekend once a month . . . for how long? Two months, maybe three? It isn't going to last—"

"Why not? For your information I'm hoping it doesn't last more than a month or two myself."

His words stung as sharply as a slap across the face.

"Maybe by that time you'll be miserable enough to be willing to marry me—"

"Marry you?" Lacey wasn't sure she'd heard him correctly, and if ever things had to be crystal clear it was now. "Of course," he snapped. "You can't honestly believe I was planning on making this commute every month for the rest of our lives, did you?"

"Well, yes, that's exactly what I thought," she whispered.

"I figured it might take a couple of miserable months apart for you to realize you love me."

"I know I love you now, you idiot.

Why else do you think I turned down a hot fudge sundae? I told you how I felt this very afternoon."

He glared at her suspiciously. "No, you didn't."

"Jack," she said impatiently, "you were driving the moving van back to the rental company, and I looked you right in the eye and said it."

"What you said was you were crazy about me. There's a world of difference between crazy and love. If you love me you're going to have to make it abundantly clear, otherwise there's going to be a problem. You already know I love you."

"No, I don't," she argued. "You've never once told me how you feel about me."

He shut his eyes as if he were seconds away from losing his patience. "A man doesn't say that sort of thing lightly, especially if the woman has only admitted to being crazy. Besides, you must know how I feel. A blind man on the street would know I've been in love with you from the moment you knocked on my door and demanded that Dog do right by Cleo."

"You . . . never said anything."

"How could I? You were as prickly as a cactus. It took me weeks to get you to agree to so much as a date. Just when I was beginning to think I was making some progress, along comes this promotion. What else am I supposed to do but pray you miss me so much you'll agree to marry me."

"I do," Lacey whispered.

Apparently Jack didn't hear her. "Another thing. You just got your raise, and I've never seen you so happy. You aren't going to want to uproot your life now, just when you've finally gotten what you wanted."

"I don't think you heard me, Jack. I said I do. Furthermore, if I've been happy lately, did it ever occur to you it might be because I'd fallen in love with you?"

"You do what?" he demanded impatiently.

"Agree to marry you. This minute. Tomorrow. Or two months down the road, whatever you want."

He squinted his eyes and stared at her as if he wasn't sure he should trust her. "What about your job?"

"I'll give two weeks' notice first thing in the morning."

"Your lease?"

"I'll sublet the place. Listen here, Jack Walker, if you think you're going to back down on your offer now, I've got a word or two for you."

He stood and walked all the way around her. "You're serious? You'd be willing to marry me just like that?"

Her grin widened, and she snapped her fingers. "Just like that. You don't honestly believe I'd let a wonderful man like you slip through my fingers, do you? I can't let you go, Jack." She threw her arms around his neck and spread happy, eager kisses all over his face.

Jack wrapped his arms around her waist and lifted her off the ground. Their kiss was slow, tender, and thorough. By the time they finished, Lacey was left weak and breathless.

"I'll never let you go, Jack Walker."

"That's more like it," he said with a

dash of male arrogance, and pulled her tightly against him again.

It was exactly where she wanted to be. Close to his heart for all time.

Cat Treats and Cat Treat Recipes

The pet stores are full of cat treats. But did you know that you can make your own healthy kitty treats at home? Here are some recipes to help you find a way to your cat's heart.

SAVORY CHEESE TREATS

¾ cup white flour
¾ cup shredded cheddar cheese
5 tablespoons grated
   parmesan cheese
¼ cup plain yogurt or sour cream
¼ cup cornmeal

Preheat the oven to 350°F. Combine cheeses and yogurt. Add flour and corn-meal. If needed, add a small amount of water to create a nice dough. Knead dough into a ball and roll to ¼ inch.

*This article has been provided courtesy of PetPlace.com (www .petplace.com), the definitive online source for pet news, health, and wellness information.

Cut into 1-inch-sized pieces and place on greased cookie sheet. Bake for 25 minutes. Makes 2 dozen.

CHICK 'N' BISCUITS

1½ cups shredded cooked chicken
½ cup chicken broth
1 cup whole wheat flour
1/3 cup cornmeal
1 tablespoon soft margarine

Preheat the oven to 350°F. Combine chicken, broth, and margarine and blend well. Add flour and cornmeal. Knead dough into a ball and roll to ¼ inch. Cut into 1-inch-sized pieces and place on an ungreased cookie sheet. Bake at 350°F for 20 minutes. Makes 18 cookies.

CRISPY LIVER MORSELS

½ cup cooked chicken livers
¼ cup water
1¼ cup whole wheat flour
¼ cup cooked carrot, mashed
1 tablespoon soft margarine

Preheat the oven to 325°F. Place well-done livers in a blender with ¼ cup water. In a bowl, combine flour and margarine. Add liver mixture and carrots and knead dough into a ball. Roll dough to ¼-inch thick and cut into 1-inch-sized pieces. Place cookies on a greased cookie sheet and bake at 325°F for 10 minutes. Makes 12 cookies.

TUNA TIDBITS

One 6-ounce can of tuna
¼ cup water drained from tuna
3 tablespoons cooked
    egg white, chopped
¼ cup cornmeal
½ cup whole wheat flour

Preheat oven to 350°F. Combine tuna, egg white, and water. Add cornmeal and flour and blend to form a dough. Knead into a ball and roll to ¼-inch thick. Cut into 1-inch-sized pieces. Bake at 350°F for 20 minutes. Makes 12 cookies.